DEADLY PURSUIT

A Western Story

DEADLY PURSUIT

A Western Story

T.V. Olsen

Thorndike Press • Chivers Press
Thorndike, Maine USA   Bath, Avon, England

This Large Print edition is published by Thorndike Press, USA and by Chivers Press, England.

Published in 1996 in the U.S. by arrangement with Golden West Literary Agency, Inc.

Published in 1996 in the U.K. by arrangement with Golden West Literary Agency.

U.S.   Hardcover   0-7862-0717-5 (Western Series Edition)
U.K.   Hardcover   0-7451-4863-8 (Chivers Large Print)
U.K.   Softcover   0-7451-4869-7 (Camden Large Print)

Thorndike Large Print ® Western Series.

The text of this Large Print edition is unabridged.
Other aspects of the book may vary from the original edition.

Set in 16 pt. News Plantin by Minnie B. Raven.

Printed in Great Britain on permanent paper.

British Library Cataloguing in Publication Data available

Library of Congress Cataloging in Publication Data

Olsen, Theodore V.
    Deadly pursuit / T.V. Olsen.
        p.   cm.
    ISBN 0-7862-0717-5 (lg. print : hc)
    1. Large type books. I. Title.
    [PS3565.L8D43   1995b]
    813'.54—dc20   95-30255

For Beverly

For Beverly

Chapter One

Noah, Noah, thought Silas Pine as he halted his piebald mount on a rise and surveyed the vast stretch of grassy bottomlands ranging below. *What am I going to tell you this time around? What the hell am I going to say, boy?*

Pine really hadn't an idea under the sun, as he gazed down at the isolated village of Grafton, nestled in a bend of the Blackbow River. From this distance it looked quaint and sequestered, a child's conception of a village created by an arrangement of alphabet blocks. All of it had been said before, and his only son had bitterly and savagely rejected his advances.

All the same he was heading for Grafton. That was where Noah was, he had only lately learned, and that's where Silas Pine had to go . . . for one last try at reconciliation with the boy.

Quit stalling, Pine told himself. *It's got to be done, so might as well get ahead with it.*

He gigged his saddle horse, attached by a rope to his pack horse, and moved on down the slope.

Neither animal was much to look at, but he hadn't been particular when he'd purchased them at a remote trader's post a week's journey to the north of here. The piebald mare was whey-bellied and slightly spavined. The bay pack horse had a sweenied shoulder that indicated an atrophied muscle and a pair of capped hips, the result probably of the hip-bones having been chipped from falls when he was being clumsily rough-broken.

Both of them were serviceable pieces of horseflesh for Silas Pine's undemanding needs, as he wasn't ordinarily a horseman anyway. His legs were powerfully muscled from years of tramping the wild mountain places, following his traplines. It was a solitary and active way of life for him and, only in recent years had it begun to pall.

Pine supposed it was largely just the ordeal of hard living, much as he loved it. And, of course, from simple aging. He'd turn fifty this autumn. A man began to feel increasingly the aches in his joints . . . and a need to slow down. That is what that Army doctor had told him after examining him and listening to his heart with a wooden stethoscope. He could hear, that doctor had said, a fleeting pericardial rub on the surface of the left ventricle. He had shown Silas an elaborate diagram of the human heart and indicated what the left ventricle was and where it was located. That there was a pericardial rub meant that he had experienced a heart attack. An "infarct" the doctor had called it and Silas insisted he write the word down so he could see it and, perhaps, better understand what he was being told. The doctor attributed this "infarct" to a fatty degeneration of the myocardium. In Silas's language, he had said, that meant basically one thing. *He might die at any moment!* He must avoid excessive physical and emotional strain. He could avoid physical strain.

But there was Noah. Dammit, he had to have one more try at making his peace with Noah.

This was a pleasant enough piece of country, Pine had to concede as he rode down the switchbacks of the undulating rises well east of the foothills of the looming Neversummer peaks. The rises enclosed the bottomlands below with a gentle splendor. The mixture of plains and dunes was mantled with scattered groves of pine and juniper whose tough, twisted roots had grasped a tenacious hold in the shallow soil.

The autumn morning was pleasant too; the late-blooming and dying grass alike was beaded with dew. Settlement of the region was widely scattered, most of the local ranches or small homesteads having their outfits located off the usual beaten paths. No doubt, they were all frontier individualists. All the same, they would appear to be pretty tame customers measured next to Silas Pine.

He wasn't what you'd call a "bear-stompin' wildcat" — his manner was quiet and reserved. Partly, maybe, because he was a late arrival in the immense territory that had once been the stamping ground of the old-time *hivernants*, the buckskin-clad mountain men who had tramped and trapped this country nearly a half century ago.

The time for whooping it up at the rip-roaring *rendezvous* of old was long past. Probably Pine wouldn't have cottoned to them anyway; a taste for solitude and personal freedom ran too deeply in his blood. Just that he had survived so lonesome and hazardous a life for so many years testified how right the choice had been for him. But his desertion of the two people to whom he was once close had taken a wicked toll on them and, in later times, on his own conscience.

Silas Pine wasn't tall, but he was as broad as a bear and almost as shaggy. His beefy chest swelled his shabby, worn buckskin jacket; his arms were long and thickly knotted with muscle. His hands were darkly brown except for a pale cording of old scars, yet they weren't large or clumsy hands. Fastened around his reins, they guided the mare with an easy sensitivity.

His long coal-black hair was tied with a thong back of his neck, and his battered slouch hat, pulled down almost to eye level, gave him a nearly sinister look from a distance. Yet a close study of his weathered face, what you could see of it above his dense and slightly grizzled beard, showed nothing at all malignant. His alert and pale blue eyes, startling in his dark face, were neither friendly nor unkind.

He had hunted often, but only for food, and he had no fondness for the meager trapping that served his equally meager needs — whatever needs the wilderness itself couldn't supply. He simply and stolidly accepted what killing he had to do as the price of living on his own terms, his own way.

Over the years Pine had killed a few men, too. He'd done it without pleasure, only for survival's sake. That was also part of his stolid philosophy. Even in the remote places, a man living by himself ran into a few mean or greedy loners who were willing to murder a man for a small cache of furs or the handful of his possessions. He had learned to keep a wary eye on strangers — and to treat them with a guarded hospitality unless they tried to get a dangerous edge on him. Once they did, it was his business to get the edge first. . . .

It was mid-afternoon when Silas Pine rode into the small village of Grafton. This was a totally unplanned hamlet, having untidily grown up one building at a time along the Blackbow's bank, with no attempt to define streets or alleys.

At first glance the place looked to be drowsing in the height of day's heat. Pine saw only a few people going about their ordinary business. Around the outskirts were ranged some squalid-looking cabins; a few women were hanging out wash or feeding chickens or exchanging gossip. Several broke off talk to stare at him, a wild-looking outlander.

Pine touched his hat briefly, politely, to each one, then rode on into the downtown or business section. It didn't amount to much: a blacksmith shop, a feed company, a couple of general merchandise stores, a small hotel with a livery barn behind it, the usual quota of saloons interspersed with whorehouses that bore names like "Jenny's Boarding Academy," and a few office buildings.

None of it caught more than Pine's surface attention. He'd seen so many similar places before. All he was really aware of was a slowly mounting tension in his gut at the prospect of meeting his son for one last attempt and being rebuffed one more time.

Maybe that's why the sudden eruption of gunshots and yelling somewhere ahead caught him totally off guard.

Pine's reaction was completely instinctive. He drummed his moccasined heels against the mare's flanks and sent the animal forward, swerving suddenly around a corner of the hotel and coming into full view of the scene.

It took Pine only a moment to realize what was happening.

A kind of open compound of trampled earth yards wide lay between buildings, and men were shooting at each other. Four of the men seemed to have scrambled out of a building that bore the legend Grafton Bank over its doorway. One of them was clutching a bulging flour sack that was maybe stuffed full of currency and gold they had lifted from the bank. Its weight would indicate something of the kind, and the difficulty it was giving the man.

This was obviously a robbery. The three men surrounding the man with the flour sack were firing back at townsmen who had probably been alerted to the robbery attempt by the explosion. As far as Pine could tell, nobody had been hit as yet on either side.

But even as Pine watched, the man clutching the flour bag toppled, both arms now pressed in toward his stomach, the flour bag dangling in front of him. He hit the ground on his face.

The others doing the shooting broke apart and ran toward horses tied at a hitching rail. One swooped up the flour bag as he ran. A lone defending townsman, well out in the open now, dropped to one knee and was systematically pumping shots at the robbers.

And one of the robbers snapped off a shot at him. It was a lucky hit. Pine saw the townsman wince, and then his head turned. His face was twisted by a grimace of pain, but Silas Pine recognized him at once. This was Noah . . . his son.

Pine had already dropped off his horse, yanking his Winchester repeater from the saddle scabbard. He cocked it and fired at the man who had wounded his son and was now aiming his six-gun to take another shot at Noah.

Silas's bullet scored a complete miss. But his bullet came close enough to the man who'd fired to make him turn, looking wildly about. Seeing Pine with a rifle trained on him, he brought his Colt .45 around in Silas's direction and sent off a hasty shot.

He missed, too.

Pine dived to the ground and flattened on his belly, his arms thrown out in front of him, fixed around the rifle, taking careful aim at the robber. He pulled the trigger. The bullet entered just above the heart, the robber being slammed backward by the slug's heavy impact. He was knocked spinning and, when he struck the ground, he rolled over twice before he lay motionless. His Colt was pinned under his body.

Pine rose shakily to his feet, seeing the blank shock of recognition on Noah's face as his bewildered glance moved from the robber's silent body to his father. Silas had just saved his son's life.

And Noah was unmistakably aware of it.

Chapter Two

Pine took his horses to the livery barn and told the freckle-faced young hostler to put them up. The youth eagerly agreed; he had been witness to the shoot-out, and now he gave Pine a slightly awed appraisal.

"You look kinda familiar," he said. "Hey, I know. You look kinda like the marshal. . . ."

"Good reason. I'm his pa."

"Wow! Honest Injun? Gee it was sure lucky for him you. . . ."

"Yeah," Pine cut in wearily, handing him the reins. "Walk my horses, water 'em, grain 'em. Can you do that?"

"Sure thing. Gee! You want to take that stuff on the pack horse along with you?"

Pine, accustomed to the remote silences of the wild, was already irritated by this kid's excited jabber. Wordlessly he turned and unfastened the diamond hitch that secured his possibles to the pack horse. He slung the pack to the ground.

"I'll leave it here for now. . . . What's your name?"

"Tip Maginnis."

"All right. Put that away for me, will you?"

"Okay, but gee! Ain't you stayin' a spell?"

"Don't know yet, Maginnis."

Pine pivoted on a heel and strode from the barn. The open area out front was almost deserted now, for nearly all the townsmen involved in foiling the robbery attempt had joined Noah in a posse that had pursued the two robbers who had managed to escape with the loot. The bodies of the two dead outlaws had been taken away.

Noah had not looked again at his father after that first shocked glance. He had simply wheeled around and bawled orders for men to form a pursuit party.

Pine had just stood flat-footed and watched as the men got their horses and galloped out of town. They would be gone a while, chasing after the two robbers who'd escaped.

All the same, Pine thought grimly, Noah would hear him out now. He was bound to after what had just happened.

Pine tramped over to the log building which combined a marshal's office with a one-cell jail. He entered the office, glanced at the jail cell, and saw it was empty. He cast his glance around the office. It was barrenly furnished with a battered desk, a swivel chair behind it, a potbelly stove, a gun rack, a narrow cot,

17

a shelf of meager grub supplies, utensils, and some dishware.

Pine slumped into the visitor's chair with a grunt, stretched out his legs and mused on what he would say to Noah when he returned. It didn't make for very optimistic thinking. They had been through it all before. Well, what the hell! There might still be a chance . . . now.

After a while he dozed in the chair and slipped gratefully into a fatigued slumber.

It was the place of the trap. A gorge of the Snake River loomed ahead, sculptured over eons by volcanic upthrusts and withering erosion and silent, encroaching glaciers. Pine knew he was riding, moving through monoliths of black lava and turrets of russet-colored sandstone, bizarre obsidian mosques tinted flaming crimson by the dying sun. Then he was no longer riding, but looking instead deeply into the gorge, a heavy mist rising from the cascading water of Twin Falls, obscuring the river with thick clouds of vapor.

The roar was incredible and it made the earth tremble, drowning out every other sound by its primeval crashing thunder as tons upon tons of water plunged downward and were lost in the engulfing spray. Before him Pine could see the grand basaltic horseshoe

18

with the driving water pouring over it, a gigantic flood of water the color of Arctic snow, smashing against the south wall of the canyon and rolling away down pale green arteries that led inexorably into the haze of foam below.

There were two boulders ahead and Pine was afoot. He had to use both his hands to keep himself from slipping off the smooth, round surfaces of the rocks, slick with spray from the pounding torrential falls. His Colt was in his holster and he dared not think about it. Once he had crawled between the two boulders, his boots slipping and sliding on the polished, wet shale beneath his feet, he paused because he could see the man standing there on a narrow ledge that jutted outward about six feet from the canyon wall, its surface glistening darkly in the fading light. The man's hands were raised and he lurched as he grabbed an outgrowth of stubborn juniper. He steadied himself. He was watching Pine as he carefully slid along the slick surface of the nearer boulder. There were ten feet between them, and the ground trembled so fitfully that it made Pine dizzy, while the roar of the falls deafened him. The man was shouting something, but Pine couldn't make it out. He shouted back and he wasn't heard. Even Pine couldn't hear his own voice.

It was then, to his terror, that Pine seemed

to soar out over the narrow defile. He was part of the cascading water now, falling swiftly toward that farther south wall, the green arteries of churning water speeding toward him. He didn't want to look down but he couldn't help himself, and he saw the erupting foam coming closer rapidly, the mist clouding his vision. Pine thought he was screaming.

The roar was gone. Instead, as he awoke, Pine could hear the sounds of riders coming into town. A glance toward the single, one-paned window told him it hadn't all been a dream. It was late afternoon and the street seemed awash with a flood of diffused, darkly wine-red light. It was close to sunset. He hitched himself up tiredly in the chair, not feeling much refreshed. It was then he noticed how he had broken out into a heavy sweat, his forehead and face drenched, his hair clinging to his scalp as if he had been soaked by the watery spray from the mighty Twin Falls.

Pine made no other move. He waited.

After maybe five minutes, Noah came tramping into the office, carrying his rifle in one hand. He halted at once, seeing his father, then closed the door and walked to the gunrack and set the rifle in it. He went over to the potbelly stove and laid a hand on the big cowcamp coffeepot.

20

"Java's still warm," he observed in a neutral voice. "You could of had some if you wanted."

"I was pretty tired," said Pine. "Plunked myself down and caught a bit o' sleep, waiting on you to come back. How's the arm?"

Apparently Noah had received only a slight flesh wound in one arm; his sleeve was rolled up and a bandanna was tied around the wrist. "Nothing," he said. "A crease is all."

He got two tin cups from the shelf and filled both from the coffeepot. He carried one cup to his father and Pine took it and drained half of it in a swallow.

"You must of left the eggshells out of this batch," he said. "Would have picked it up a mite."

"I reckon," Noah said in the same colorless, guarded way. He took a swig of the weak and sorry brew, then set the cup down on the desk and slung one hip over the corner of it, punching his hat back on his brow, eyeing Silas warily.

"Catch up with those two?" Pine asked.

Noah moved his head left to right. "They got clean away. We'll have to track them down, but it's too late in the day. We'll pick up the trail tomorrow."

"That's only good sense."

"I owe you now," Noah said roughly. "All right. What d'you want of me?"

21

"The same old thing," Pine said. "You know what that is. But you always hated me too much to care. Thought maybe you would, now."

Noah laughed shortly, bitterly. "Like you thought you'd have a chance to save my hide when you rode into Grafton."

"No," Silas Pine said patiently. "No way a man could know that. It just happened. You've heard all I had to say before. It's up to you, Noah."

Scowling, Noah paced a slow circle in the office, running a hand through his shock of thick black hair. Unlike his father's, it tended to grow out in big loppy curls — rather like his mother's — and his square young face lacked the still and stubborn set of Silas's. It was more animated, showing all the cross-currents of his feelings. He was big-boned and about Silas's height, though not as thickly built. Likely that would come with time. Otherwise, their father-son tie was pretty evident.

"Ahhh . . . !" Noah dropped into his swivel chair and eyed his father in a cold, baffled way. "I already said it. I owe you. You mind bedding down in the cell?" He tipped his head toward the cot. "That's my bed . . . haven't much to accommodate a visitor. But the cell bunk has it all over anything in that ratty local hotel of ours."

"Sure. It'll be fine."

"All right. You got any possibles along?"

"Left 'em at the stable."

"Bring 'em here. Then we'll go have some supper and talk a spell." Noah added almost grudgingly, "I reckon it's time we did."

Over supper at the local restaurant, they did talk, and both men were uncomfortable. But their arid and somewhat strained conversation did offer them a little more knowledge about each other. Pine realized fully and sadly how far he and Noah had really fallen apart over the years.

"One thing I never told you before," Silas said. "I married again. It was quite a while after I left you and your mother. She was a Navajo woman. We lived with her band for a time, but mostly we lived by ourselves."

Looking down at his plate, Noah shook a dusting of salt and pepper over the thick steak and the mound of fried potatoes he'd ordered. Then he glanced up and said tonelessly, "Yeah, you would. Did you desert her too?"

"No," Pine said, iron-voiced. "I didn't have anything to do with white folks any more, so it didn't seem improper to marry her in the Navajo way. She died about a year and a half after. Came down with the white man's pox." He hesitated. "Didn't seem to touch me, not that I know of. But by then I was doing some trading with whites. Could be I fetched it to her, unknowing. You must know how that sort o' thing takes Indians off."

"Yeah. Did you beget any . . . offspring?"

"No. She left me no issue. You're all I got left now."

He half expected an icy repudiation, but Noah merely grunted, picked up his knife and fork and cut into the meat. Pine began to carve up his own steak. He put a hunk in his mouth, chewed and thought it was a choice cut, then spoke around it.

"How about you? Got yourself a girl yet?"

"Kind of, I guess." Noah almost smiled, then vaguely stirred the air with his fork. "There's a girl I been courting, daughter of Horace Rogan's housekeeper — Rogan's the owner of the bank. Susan's her name. She works for Ma at the little trading post Ma has across from the Gold Bar Saloon. But I want to wait on marriage. This marshal job . . . it might just be temporary. Not sure I'd care to stick with it a whole lifetime."

"You're looking ahead. Wish I'd done more of it when I was your age."

"Well, you didn't," Noah said matter-of-factly. "And that's that."

"All right. I just wish I could do it over."

"Forget it, Pa."

This was the first time his son had acknowledged him as *father* since Noah was a child. Pine was inordinately pleased, but decided it would be wiser not to comment. In silence they finished their meals and had the waitress fetch them second cups of coffee.

Silas wiped his napkin across his mouth and picked up his cup. If the two of them did any more talking right now, likely it would be better to change the subject.

"I'm wondering about those fellows who went after the bank today," he said. "Were they strangers to you . . . just ne'er-do-wells passing through?"

Noah sipped his own coffee, then shook his head. "They was all locals. Jake Milton, Asa Blayde . . . those were the ones we got. You gunned down Blayde. All of them were shoestring ranchers out in the valley. The two who got away were Ben Massingale and Sam Crowley, a black man."

"How come they took to holding up the bank?"

"Shouldn't be too hard to guess." Noah showed a fleeting and crooked smile. "They were all desperate for money."

"Things that bad hereabouts?"

"For the little guy, sure. Ain't it always?"

"Most times, it seems to be," Pine said slowly. "But saying so kind of puts you at

25

odds with your sworn duty, don't it?"

Noah nodded wryly and sighed. "That's the way the world is, Pa. I didn't make it that way. But it's still my job to run 'em down."

"That's another thing you learned pretty young, then."

"I guess so." Noah gazed glumly at the red-and-white-checked tablecloth. "Anyway . . . it's been really bad for them the last few years. I'd hazard that's why those four threw in together for this robbery. I suppose they figured on clearing out of the country right afterward, along with their families."

"And you said you'll be picking up those two men's trails tomorrow?"

"That's right. At first light of dawn. A goodly number of the townsmen have said they'll be willing to go on posse with me again."

Pine gently cleared his throat. "You think you could maybe use a good guide on track? I might serve."

"I reckon you'd be a damned good hand on trailin'." Again Noah's neutral, guarded tone. "You had a good many years living that way."

"I did. And can likely do as well for you as anyone else in any kind o' wild country. That's if you'd want me along."

Noah's gaze swung up. Suddenly and surprisingly, his mouth broke into a full and engaging grin. "I do." He reached a hand across the table. "Shake on it?"

Pine's hand gripped his son's; he felt a quick stinging in his eyes. And he had the startling thought that the old breach between them had been healed all at once. Cleanly healed.

Chapter Three

No sunup yet. Only a pale amethyst hint of dawn showed as the party of a dozen men, led by Silas and Noah Pine, rode north out of Grafton. They formed black barely-seen cutouts of mounts and riders as they clopped softly along the bends of a road that was little more than a dusty trail. The wind was back, however, tugging and pulling at their clothes, their hats, the manes of the horses. The wind that almost never ceased and which had, for some reason, been absent the previous day. It made a soft purring sound that was only subliminally perceptible most of the time because its presence was so habitual, except when it had been silent for a time and, then, came back.

Pine made no effort as yet to follow track. The robbers' hoofprints had been trampled and obliterated by the pursuit party yesterday. When they came to where that aborted trail ended, he could pick up on the earlier sign, and by then there should be light enough by which to see.

So he and Noah, out ahead of the others,

talked idly in quiet voices. Pine relished this new, easier feeling between them, even if both still showed some residual caution in their speech.

"You want to know something about the boys with us?" Noah asked. "I introduced you all around, but that don't tell anything. Myself, I always like to know more. Can be useful to know who's backing you."

The wind restlessly pulled at Noah's words, but Silas could hear them all right and he thought, *We're a team, him and me.* It was a strangely warm feeling that spread within him. One he'd never felt with any man before. He was that much of a born loner. "Sure," he rasped into the wind. "Go ahead."

"Well . . . ," Noah jerked his head in a small backward motion, "that squat old fellow with the muttonchop whiskers, he's Horace Rogan, president of our little bank. His son, Obbie, was one of his clerks. Obbie got shot dead yesterday when they braced him and he came up with a gun instead of the cash they asked for. That shot was what alerted the rest of us."

Pine nodded. The stocky Rogan's hair was totally gray, but he'd felt the power in the old man's grip when they'd shaken hands earlier, and he'd noted the bulldog squint to the banker's eyes and mouth. Something was riding him powerfully hard.

"Then there's Isom Rastrow," Noah went on. "Him and them four riding alongside are horse-hunters. They just happened in town, buying some grub, about two weeks ago and have been hanging around ever since. Rastrow was mustanging for years in the Twin Falls region in Idaho. He says it's all mustanged out which is why he came here. He wants to try his hand at horse ranching instead."

"I can believe Twin Falls is mustanged out," Pine said. "It sure is trapped out. I was just in that area before I decided to come back to Wyoming. I wanted to see you. I felt sick a lot of the time and I've had a bad dream."

"A bad dream?" Noah asked.

"Yes, and the Twin Falls are in it. That's one of the reasons I felt I had to get out of there and stay away."

"Rastrow's is a hardcase lot, all of them, and like to sniff out trouble," Noah went on. "They follow trouble like hound dogs on scent. That's why they came along, that and the fact that Rastrow seems to have become rather thick with Rogan. The two siding Rastrow are Reno Poteet and Bruno Banes, and bringing up the rear Black Ellis and Lefty Price."

Pine nodded. He knew which men Noah meant (none had offered to shake hands) and he'd at once assessed them as a trail-hardened and roughshod I-don't-give-a-damn crew, like lobo wolves banding together in common likeness. He had plenty of lobo in his own nature, but generally he didn't take to the breed. Most of them seemed whelped mean, as if meanness were bred in the bone.

Maybe he was just prejudiced against all horse-hunters. They'd go to any lengths to run down wild mustangs, rough-break them and sell them to the first bidder, to be used for any purpose. Pine had an instinctive sympathy for all wild animals.

He said bluntly, "I don't much like their kind, Noah."

"Didn't figure you would. Neither do I." Noah's expression was almost hidden in the half-dark, but Pine caught the faint flash of his grin. "The rest of 'em, now. . . ."

Pine mentally reviewed the appearances of the other men as Noah ticked off a short description of each one. The blacksmith, a couple teamsters, a saloon bouncer, and a lone shopkeeper. With the exception of the banker, they were all single men, with no family responsibilities. They comprised a tough-looking lot who had been likely lured most by the prospect of having the fun of quitting the drudgery of their jobs for a spell and seeing some risky action. In other words, a sound crew of men to have backing you on a gritty expedition.

He was impressed, too, by the way his son, younger than any of them, had taken these men under his leadership. They respected Noah, by God.

I never gave him a damn thing to look up to, Pine reflected. *He won it all on his own. You sired yourself a prize pup, you old bastard, even if you never earned it. . . .*

As daylight grew and a warming sun touched their right sides, Noah called a halt at the spot where darkness had forced them to abandon the trail yesterday.

"Maybe we can save some time," he told them. "I want to have a look at those men's places — Massingale's and Crowley's. Damn small odds we'll find either of 'em at home, but we might learn something."

The posse proceeded a little farther on the road, then cut away from it toward the northwest. They pushed through dense timber for an hour, escaping the lagging power of the wind which blew more freely in the open areas, and emerged onto a mixture of grassy hills and flats. The wind found them again, rushing through the waves of grass and flattening it atop the hills. Ahead, presently, they saw a crude layout of log buildings some distance away. Smoke was spiraling up from a chimney before the wind caught it and sent it in billows that seemed to evaporate. But they could smell it as they approached.

"That's Massingale's place, and it seems somebody's home," Noah said and raised his hand for a halt, looking at his father. "You find something, Pa?"

Pine had dropped off his horse and was down on one knee, inspecting the sparse grass and ground. "They came out of the woods pretty close to here. Their horses trampled the grass and clay some."

Noah peered down, then shook his head with a chuckle. "I'd never of made that out. All right, men, if Pa says so, they came here. Move on, now. Keep your guns to hand, but take it slow. We'll be in the open all the way. And don't pull iron except on my order."

They spread out a little as they rode forward, some easing their revolvers and rifles in their scabbards, but not taking them out. The persistent wind continued to break the spiral of cabin smoke into chinked tatters.

Pine saw now that a well-traveled dirt road ran crookedly from north to south, transecting the long flatland in front of the cabin. He asked Noah about it.

"Stage route," Noah explained. "Swings so far east of Grafton that the stage company asked Massingale if they could re-route it past

33

his place and have him serve as station master. He was more'n willing to take the position."

"And that brings him in some extra money?"

"Not near enough for his needs," Noah clarified. "It ain't what you'd call a great paying proposition."

The men were braced for some possible gunfire, but it didn't happen. Some hundred feet from the cabin, Noah halted the men again and raised his voice in a yell: *"Halloo, the house!"*

There was no answer. But the cabin door was prodded partly open. A rifle barrel emerged first and then the door opened fully and the woman came out, holding the rifle half-leveled.

She was an eyeful, for sure. A rather short but sturdy and well-curved woman in her mid-thirties. Not what you'd call pretty, too round-faced for that, but nice-looking all the same, with those vivid blue eyes and the untidy mass of flaming-red hair pinned atop her head. Her drab gray linsey dress may have fitted her badly, puckering and collapsing in the wind, but her vivacious femininity struck a man like a physical blow.

"And what will ye be wanting here, scuts!" She almost spat the words.

"You know well enough, ma'am," Noah

said gently. "I'd point that piece farther downward if I was you. Trying to use it will get you nowhere. Except it could get you hurt."

"So . . . ye'd throw down on a woman then, bucko lad?"

"If I got shot at first and I came out alive, I just might, yes, ma'am."

Slowly and grudgingly, she let the rifle muzzle settle till it nearly touched the ground. "Very well. Say what ye want. Then clear out, the lot of ye."

"We'll have to search this place first, Miss Shawn. To be sure your husband or Crowley aren't here."

A small bitter smile shaped her wide full lips. "Go ahead, then, and the devil take ye. I can say, for your convenience, that there's naebody here." Her strong combination Scottish and Irish brogue seemed to slacken only slightly as her temper eased.

"But they have been?"

"I'll leave ye to guess about that, ye shrewd young deputy."

The men dismounted at Noah's order; they fanned out among the buildings. Noah himself, along with Silas, undertook a search of the small cabin.

The log house consisted of only two rooms, the front one containing a fieldstone fireplace and a trestle table and a meager stock of provisions. The room behind it contained the sleeping quarters: a wide double bed and a narrow cot, both hand-hewn from split logs. Everything looked very plain, but all of it was scrupulously clean.

A quite pretty red-haired girl of eleven or twelve was sitting on the cot, hugging her drawn-up knees. Her eyes were dark and wide and scared.

Noah gave the room a circling glance, then smiled at the girl. "It's all right, Kerry Lu. We're about to leave."

The men hadn't found anyone in the outbuildings. There were a couple of lathered horses that had been tended and left in the corral. Pine followed the tracks of two fresh horses, obviously exchanged for the first pair, out to the yard. He followed the tracks a little farther, then nodded toward the northwest.

"Different direction now," Silas concluded. "But they're on a straight line, looks like."

"They're headed for Crowley's, then," said Noah. "They'll have packed along some grub, isn't that right, Miss Shawn?"

The woman had laid down her rifle on the porch. She stood now with fists planted on her hips, eyeing them scornfully. "Enough to last for days. And they'll get more at Sam's place. Ye'll ne'er catch 'em." Her bleak blue

36

gaze shuttled to Silas Pine. "That leather-clad spalpeen. He your daddy? Looks to be."

"Yes. And a handy man on trail, Miss Shawn."

"Looks that, too. Ye must of combed him out of the brush."

"He combed himself out pretty well," Noah said good-humoredly. "Your husband will have to go some to stay ahead of him."

"Ay, that he will," Shawn Massingale said confidently. "Both of 'em will."

"Remains to be seen."

"Devil your luck, young man!"

Noah touched his hat and told the men to mount up again. They rode north across the short grass, Pine casting a final glance back at Miss Shawn still standing with fists on her hips, glaring after them. Then Kerry Lu came out of the cabin and stood beside her mother, who put an arm around her shoulders.

"That's a mighty tough lady," Pine observed. "Out of the old country, eh?"

"Straight from Erin's green isle for her ma and Glasgow for her pa," Noah said. "It's a sad case, Pa. As I understand it, she and Massingale met in Boston, and neither of 'em had any money or any kin — outside of that young girl of theirs, now. But they got married, threw in together to come out here and try their fortunes." Noah sighed inaudibly in the wind, shaking his head. "Some fortune. . . ."

Silas listened, grateful now for the wind, since it dried the perspiration which otherwise would have been literally dripping from his face. He felt a faint sense of nausea and a deep weariness had settled into his joints. He hadn't told Noah, yet. It could wait. In fact, what did it matter . . . ?

In maybe another hour, they reached Crowley's place, taking the same precautions about approaching it. As before, they met no opposition. Compared to the Massingale cabin, here was a real hardscrabble outfit, with a single tiny log shack for the house, and a couple makeshift, rather ramshackle outsheds.

Noah spoke briefly with Crowley's wife, a young, thin, sullen-faced black woman in a frayed dress. She stared at them with total hostility while she patted the back of a baby with the hiccups slung against her left breast and shoulder. She was no more cooperative than Shawn Massingale had been, although she had none of Miss Shawn's bright and biting sarcasm to offer. Plainly, all she wanted was to have them away from here.

As the posse rode off, Pine murmured, "I got no cause to be proud of myself. But whenever I see what we done to colored folks. . . ."

"That's right, Pa," Noah nodded. "None of us got a whit to be proud of. You just get us back on track again."

Chapter Four

Pine had no trouble following the fresh trail of the fugitives. Most of the time he rode steadily at the front of the posse, merely bending out of his saddle to survey the ground. A few times he had to dismount and study the track more closely.

The posse wasn't moving at any great pace, and some of the men were growing restless. There was some grumbling or talk of abandoning the chase. One man who didn't complain at all, who never said a word, was Horace Rogan, riding stone-faced and silent. But nobody went so far as actually to drop out. They realized that Silas Pine's guidance was enabling them to go a good deal faster than otherwise — that without his assistance they might easily lose the trail altogether.

By sunset, they drew up just short of the Neversummer foothills and pitched camp. Noah warned the men not to light any fires. They didn't need the warmth in this mild weather and the fire-glow might get the attention of the two fugitives, if they weren't far ahead.

"They won't reckon us to be this close be-hind 'em even if they reckon we're after 'em," Noah told the men. "Eat whatever food you packed along. Do without coffee. I'm gam-bling we can catch up with 'em early to-morrow."

There was more grumbling, but they saw the sense of it. However Isom Rastrow and his horse-hunting companions, Poteet, Ellis, Price, and Banes, were on the edge of a rising. One of them broke out a bottle and all of them shared it, passing it around as the other posse men sat tiredly on their heels in the growing dusk, munching whatever food they had along. Everyone was pretty quiet, or speaking in *soto voce* murmurs, with the exception of Rastrow and his crew.

Sitting apart with his son, Pine nodded to-ward the boisterous crew and said: "There's trouble. Just one bad card in a deck can do. Five is worse than bad."

"I only hope they don't cut loose soon," Noah said, chewing on a cold sandwich and washing it down with canteen water. "We're real close to Massingale and Crowley. Have a feeling in my bones about it. We don't keep reasonably quiet, it could throw 'em on guard."

Pine nodded and was about to reply when one of Rastrow's men got up and came toward

41

them. Pine couldn't make him out clearly in the thickening dusk, but knew from his thick build and stumpy rolling stride that this was Bruno Banes.

Banes was weaving unsteadily, already several sheets to the wind.

"Careful now," Pine warned Noah, and rose to his feet.

Banes pulled up about four yards away, his legs set apart. He hesitated and then spoke, his voice blurred by drink. "Hey there, you scraggle-faced ol' deputy's pa. You aim to brace me?"

"No," Pine said quietly, almost impersonally. "Just wondered what's on your mind." He managed not to add, *if you have one.*

Bruno Banes hiccoughed and laughed. "Well, you air packin' a smokepole. So am I." His hand almost brushed the holstered gun at his hip. "We can try conclusions right here 'n' now."

"No."

"Huh? What's 'at you say?"

"I say no. You're drunk as a skunk. I never cold-blooded shot any man. But you pull on me and I'll put you down faster than a hungry weasel 'ud gobble up a shrew."

"Ahhh . . . !"

"Bruno."

That was Isom Rastrow. He had a sharp,

rather thin voice, and now he and the others were on their feet. Noah stood up too, silently siding his father, saying nothing.

"Let it alone," Rastrow said, sounding fairly sober. "Never could hold your likker. Just simmer down."

"I don't like this buckskin bastard's looks," Banes said, his tone low and wicked. "Didn't from the start."

"So you said before," Rastrow answered. "Now you slack off, hear me?" His thin voice held a surprising note of authority.

Banes grunted. He stood swaying on his feet for a few seconds, then turned slowly and heavily tramped back to his companions.

The men had fallen into a tense silence when the confrontation had begun. Now, gradually, their voices picked up again. Silas and Noah relaxed slowly, sitting back once more on their haunches.

"Whee-oo." Noah's mouth, unseen in the enveloping near dark, held a smiling note. "Pa, you spiked his gun almighty well."

"I had to learn how, long time back."

"I bet you did. But you ever run into that prime specimen again, you best never put your back to him."

All that Pine had done was try to stand between Bruno Banes and whatever the drunken man might have tried to do — not to him,

43

but to his son. Yet, there seemed no point in saying as much aloud.

That night, as he slept restlessly alongside Noah, it came to Silas with a stealthy tread, laying hold of him inexorably. The same recurring dream. *The place of the trap.* Once more he was riding through those monoliths of black lava and those turrets of russet-colored sandstone forming bizarre obsidian mosques so tinted by the dying sun that they flamed darkly like viscid blood. When he suddenly was no longer riding, he was looking instead into the gorge of Twin Falls, a heavy mist rising as the water roared and plunged, the lower river obscured by thick clouds of vapor.

The earth was trembling with the roar, the thunder of it filling Pine's ears like rushing blood exploding through his veins. Before him he could see the gigantic horseshoe of basalt with the driving water pounding over it, a great flood of water the color of Arctic snow, icily forbidding, terrifying. It smashed against the south wall of the canyon only to roll away down pallid green arteries and to vanish into the haze of roiling foam below.

The man was standing there on that narrow ledge jutting outward about six feet from the stone wall of the canyon, its surface in the

44

fading light glistening. Try as he might, Pine could not recognize the man. Slipping and slithering across the wet boulder, deafened by the roar of the falls, Pine could not make out what the man was shouting. And, then, to his horror, Pine was soaring out over the narrow defile, part of the plunging, cascading water now, falling swiftly, desperately toward that farther southern wall.

Next morning, as soon as it was light enough for Silas to read sign, they set out on the trail again. Even in this dismal light, Noah could discern a bluish hue to his father's features, and he thought perhaps he was cold, although it did not seem so to him, just damp with the usual morning dew that made the joints stiff and slowed the body. Silas denied he was cold. When his son saw him then brush aside perspiration with a rapid jerk of his sleeve, he wondered if perhaps his father was suffering from some kind of fever.

Noah refused to probe the matter further, however. The trail they were following was leading them onto the lower foothills of the Neversummers and it was evident that the two fugitives had set themselves a fairly hard pace. As the sun rose higher in the sky, Noah opined that at some point those two were going to decide that it was safe to slow down. Surely the wear and tear on their horses had to be taken into account.

What they couldn't have foreseen was having on their heels a tracker of Silas Pine's ability. But they'd realize the posse must be getting close by now. Silas assured Noah of that much just by reading their sign.

"How far you reckon they're ahead, Pa?" Noah asked then.

"I'd say about two hours in time, maybe four hours in distance," Pine replied. "They're moving up to higher ground. That could give 'em some'at of an edge. Depends on how they take advantage of it."

"How's that?"

"Well, if they're up above us, they would be in good position to shoot down at us. Could roll rocks down too."

Noah said, half-grinning, "I always understood the man firing from up above wasn't as likely to hit a target as the man shooting from below."

"You understood right," Pine agreed. "Don't know why that is, but it don't change some other way they could get at us easier from above than shootin'."

Not hurrying, they moved on, Pine keeping his senses at a hair-trigger alert now. The mountainous terrain was largely a mix of boulder fields and stands of pine. Advancing, the

46

possemen held to thick cover wherever they could. It was becoming more difficult, though, all the time.

About mid-morning they came to an abrupt upslant that climbed to a tall rim standing out, sharp and irregular, against the sky. Earlier, that sky had been daubed with a few fleecy white clouds. Now, driving at them from above, tossed on the perpetually blowing wind, those clouds had deepened into thick billows, murky and ominous.

"Damn," muttered Noah, "that's just what we need. A good hard storm to wipe out. . . ."

"Wait." Pine lifted a hand sharply. "You hear that?"

"What?"

"A horse whickered up there . . . right ahead of us."

Noah shook his head, baffled. "I didn't hear. . . ."

"We're near onto 'em. So we better move fast now. Track could get wiped out. Then we may not get another chance."

Thunder rumbled gently as the riders surged up the steep incline, disregarding the risk of being spotted. They couldn't yet actually see the fugitives. But Pine's keen hearing had picked out the exact source of the sound, and he took a reckless lead ahead of his son and the others.

Now he caught a hint of movement ahead through the brush.

That meant Massingale and Crowley had picked them out too, and were urging their mounts on and upward. They hadn't ventured to go ahead too quickly before, but now they were on the run, the enemy breathing down their necks.

It brought them into the open, and the posse began firing as the first fat globules of rain began to fall.

One of the fleeing men's horses was hit. It stumbled and went down, throwing the rider. The other man looked back and hollered something, probably a curse, then wheeled back to his companion, reaching down a hand to swing him up behind him even as the man floundered to his feet.

He didn't quite make it. He jerked violently as a bullet struck him. And jerked again as a second slug hit him. Then he went down.

The other rider shrilled another curse, then reached down and whipped his rifle from its scabbard.

A jagged ribbon of lightning tore across the sky, illumining the rider's contorted face as he opened up with his repeater at the posse, sending off shots as fast as he could, their crackling echoes half lost in the sullen, droning boom of thunder.

48

Somebody behind Pine gave a painful grunt. Silas turned his head to see Noah, only a few yards distant, slip heavily from his saddle and pitch forward on his face.

For a moment Pine was frozen and unbelieving. Then he dropped off his mount and ran to his son.

Oh God . . . Noah!

He knew even before he knelt and rolled Noah's body over onto its back. The bullet had ranged down through his son's neck and emerged from between the shoulders.

One of the other posse men had been hit too. He was letting out wordless shrieks, but Pine hardly heard them or the continuing fusillade of shots being fired by the posse up ahead.

Then his frozen feeling died in a blaze of rage. He pivoted to his feet and ran to his horse, wrenching his own rifle free of its sheath. He brought it up shoulder-level as the storm suddenly unleashed its fury.

The unnatural gloom that had already stolen the daylight dimmed away as the remaining light almost completely vanished in the torrents of water cascading down. Pine was shooting wildly and insensately at where he'd last glimpsed the rider above. But he was blinded as much by the rain pelting sharply into his face as the enveloping darkness that had descended.

Then another ripple of lightning silhouetted the rider above, pushing his horse to the last rise of rimrock. Pine got off two shots before his vision was wiped out again when the shroud of darkness returned.

God damn!

The other men had quit shooting now.

Slowly and heavily, Silas Pine plodded up the slope to the body of the fallen fugitive. He stared down at it. Crowley, the black man. He had taken one bullet in the middle; the other had smashed through the back of his head. And little remained of his face.

Pine continued slogging up to the rim, with a grim foreboding of what he would find.

Nothing.

Massingale had gotten away over the rim. He was lost somewhere there on the dark slope above, amid the heavy brush and glistening rocks. The pelting rain continued to beat down savagely. All sign of his tracks would be gone.

Chapter Five

Silas Pine hunkered in the nest of heat-reflecting boulders where he was laid up in the naked midday sun. It was a miserable place to stay crouched for hours, rifle cradled in his lap. He had to be careful not to let his body touch any of the surrounding surfaces of blazing-hot rock.

But no other place was available where he could have the best vantage of the Massingale outfit down below without being spotted by anybody nearby, either by chance or by accident.

The problem was that Massingale's place lay in an area that was open on all sides. Pine couldn't range in closer without the risk of being seen. What he did have was the fathomless patience of a man trained to wilderness ways. It inured him to all discomfort, even the terrific heat and being stuck in one position for interminable lengths of time.

He had kept the vigil for nearly a week, enduring both the super-heated days and chilly nights. From time to time, he snatched a few bites of food or a few swallows of water from his canteen, but these he could keep close beside him without leaving his post. Once in a while he'd leave it in order to relieve himself or to tend his horses. Or, he'd have to break vigil at odd times just to catch a few winks of sleep.

So there were a few obvious chances for him to miss Massingale if the man did return to his little outfit, particularly at night when darkness would cover his approach. Pine had an iron confidence that Massingale would eventually return here. Certainly his wife was deeply committed to him, and no doubt his daughter too. They would not abandon him, nor he them.

Besides, where would they go? The place provided them with at least a meager living. Two stage runs would stop here daily, and Mrs. Massingale always assisted with the team changes and fed the passengers. Between times, she was busy out in her large truck garden at the back, planting and cultivating and weeding, as well as attending to the animals in the stable and pasture. In the time he had been keeping his vigil, Pine had seen only one visitor stop at the cabin, an old Mexican with a blue sash and battered sombrero. He had stayed about an hour and then ridden on toward town.

Pine had long watched Shawn Massingale,

sometimes through his field glasses, and he never tired of the watching. Shawn Massingale moved with a fluid full-bodied grace that might take a man's eye forever. It set up uncomfortable stirrings in him and he tried to ignore them. Women, outside of his brief marriage to Sah-Nee, a Navajo, had been alien to his whole experience for too many years. . . .

During the few days since Noah's death, Silas Pine had gone over and over in his mind, maybe until it had clouded his judgment, all that had led up to his present impasse. Sometimes he dimly thought that he'd saddled himself with more blame than he rightly deserved. Yet that's how it finally all added up.

It began to seem as though every act to which he'd committed himself in his whole life had led up to the death of his only son. No matter that he'd never intended it to happen. It was done.

The worst of it was the agony of having at last, after so many years, found an acceptance by Noah . . . only to lose him almost at once. Pine had needed an outlet for his seething rage and despair, and it was impossible for his mind really to function beyond that basic fact. Maybe, too, he was being assailed by his past sense of guilt for having deserted his wife and son the way he had.

He and the other men had taken Noah's body back to Grafton, where it was interred in the small cemetery. He had dully listened to the circuit preacher intone a service at the graveside without really hearing the words. He'd met the attractive girl that Noah had been courting, Susan Gates, heard her sobbing acknowledgment that she had loved his son, and that had barely registered either.

By now his mind was focused solely on one thought. He was going to get Ben Massingale, no matter what it took, or how long. Obscurely (but always fighting back the thought) he knew that Massingale was only accidentally to blame for Noah's death. All the same he had pulled the trigger; he had fired the lethal bullet.

Armed with that certain knowledge, Pine had all the focus he needed for his rage.

He didn't know whether, if it came to that, he would kill the man. He wouldn't let his thoughts range that far ahead. Could be he'd only capture him and bring him in. When a man's brain was capable of feeling nothing but a numb animal hurt, that alone could become an obsession with him. . . . He couldn't remember dreaming the nightmare which had been haunting him before Noah was shot. Perhaps he dreamt it without knowing. Or maybe he was sleeping too little to dream. If that dreadful dream came back, once this was all over, Pine had decided he would have to pay a visit to old Adakhai's camp. The Navajo shaman would be able to tell him what it meant, if anyone could. As it was, he felt no pain anywhere, and no excitement, just a soul-weariness and a grim determination.

Well back beyond the rise, Pine had a sparse camp in a jackpine grove with a small stream running through it. From time to time he would descend to it and tend his horses.

At the end of this day, probably feeling so exhausted from another long and fruitless vigil, he went down to the grove, led the horses to the stream and let them drink. Then he cooked up enough grub to last him for three more days.

That night he slept much longer than he'd intended. He'd rolled into his blankets before it was completely dark. When he woke with a start, the sun was well up and he didn't awaken naturally. It had come in response to a nearby roar of gunfire . . . several rifles going off at the same time.

Pine grabbed up his own piece before he lunged to his feet and headed for the place where the sounds of the shots were coming. The Massingale place.

Before he got clear of the jackpine grove, he heard a noise from the crackling brush along its edge and a girl's wild, half-strangled sobbing. Then she burst into sight. It was the Massingale child, and most of her clothing had been torn away, the rest hanging in tatters.

Just a few yards behind her was Bruno Banes. His face wore a look of insatiable lust.

Seeing Pine, the girl pulled up with a stifled gasp of increased panic. But suddenly then, as if instinctively and impulsively, she stumbled forward toward him, crying, "Help me, Mister! For God's sake, help me!"

Banes was a little behind her, not quite in line, and he was as surprised as she was. He braced to a thick-legged stop and grabbed for his holstered revolver with a half-crazed grunt.

Pine tipped up his rifle. What he'd just seen was enough to hold him against any such foolishness as a warning word. He simply cocked the rifle and fired from the hip, the bullet pumping audibly into Banes's heavy gut.

Banes grunted again and stumbled backward, still trying to yank his revolver clear of the holster. Pine cocked and fired again.

Banes was slammed over on his back. Blood sprayed from his mouth, hard-driven by his dying breath.

That was all.

Pine walked over to make sure of him.

Kerry Lu Massingale shrank to one side as he approached where she was standing, her eyes shining with terror, both hands pressed tightly over her mouth.

Pine bent above Banes, pulled his pistol from the holster and flung it away into the brush. Then he straightened up wearily, keeping his eyes averted from Kerry Lu. "You stay here," he told her. "I'll get you something to wear."

He tramped back to his camp and dug out his old slicker from his gear. He returned to where Kerry Lu was still standing and thrust the heavy rubberized garment toward her. "Get that on you. Then tell me what's going on."

She had remained exactly where he'd left her, as if paralyzed in place, hands pressed toward her face. Moving very slowly, she hesitantly took the slicker and managed to fumble it on around her body and to button it. She was almost lost in its folds, the skirt dragging on the ground around her feet.

"What's going on?" Pine repeated patiently.

Kerry Lu looked at him only half-comprehendingly, then broke into a torrent of speech. Pine couldn't make much out of it except that her mother was shooting it out with a couple of men. That would be either Isom Rastrow or others of his crew, Pine thought grimly. He could still hear the sporadic roar of rifle fire. But why had it happened?

"Look," he told the girl, "you just follow me, all right? I'll see if I can help your ma."

He slogged out of the grove, glancing back now and then to be sure Kerry Lu was behind him. She was, but she was staying several scary-eyed yards distant.

Pine felt an immense physical exhaustion tugging leadenly at his feet as he tramped on up the stony slope. The past week had taken a miserable toll on his energy, if not his savage and single-minded resolve to find Ben Massingale.

They passed over the slope and worked slowly down its other side, clinging to whatever cover and rocks and brush they could find. Pine couldn't tell much from his few glimpses of what was going on below, but he could see that a man was laid up behind a boulder, firing intermittently in to the cabin, and that its occupant was firing back at him.

When they reached the bottom of the incline, Pine told Kerry Lu to crouch down and lie low while he tried to get behind the man attacking the cabin. She did not indicate her understanding by a word or even a nod, but she did sink down obediently on her heels.

Pine took his time circling his way around

back of where the billows of gunsmoke were issuing; they came from a separate cluster of rock that was maybe fifty feet from the cabin. And he noted the two horses that were ground-hitched behind some boulders a little distance from the man.

In virtually total silence Pine stole up toward the man as soon as he came into view. His back was to him, and his attention was wholly on the cabin.

He edged up until he was only a few yards behind him. Then he used a moment's lull in the firing to lever his rifle. The sound was sharp and very specific.

Reno Poteet turned his head toward Pine, startled. He began to swivel around on his heels.

"Don't do that," Pine said flatly. "Stay like you are, just as you are. Throw out your long piece. Your sidearm, too. Then stand up."

Poteet's gaunt, saturnine face was making an effort to show nothing, and he did as he was told.

"Get your hands up a ways," Pine said. "Then turn around slow."

Poteet did.

"I heard a couple of shots over yonder," Poteet said phlegmily, swallowing hard in his attempt to conceal his anger.

Pine gently hefted his rifle. "They come

from this. Your friend Banes, he's bought the farm."

"Jesus!"

"My sentiments," Pine said in a deadly tone, "when I saw what he'd done to that little girl."

What little color there was had left Poteet's face, a kind of neutral caution touching it now. "I had nothing to do with that. I. . . ."

"No. You just let it happen. All he got to do was tear her clothes off. Then he pulled down on me after I give him fair warning." Pine paused. "Good thing that's all he got to do. Or I'd give you what I give him. Where's Rastrow and the others? The whole lot of you, you're a pack of triple-ply bastards if I ever seen any."

"Acting Marshal Rastrow stayed in town."

Silas grunted in disgust, glanced around toward the cabin, and yelled.

"Miz Massingale! This is Silas Pine. Noah Pine's pa. I got this pair in hand. You can come out now."

Chapter Six

It was a well-appointed room with high casement windows. The spacious clapboard house was set well back on its city lot so that one great ash tree and an elm spread their limbs widely over the front yard, shading the broad front porch and keeping the parlor dark even on the sunniest day. Antimacassars delicately crocheted by Sarah Rogan in happier days protected the backs of chairs with wooden arms and the sofa placed before the flagstone fireplace. There was a small fire in the grate and the snapping of a knot in the fir used for firewood sounded disjointedly against the steady background of the ticking of the Seth Thomas clock on the mantel and the muffled sobs of the woman in black taffeta seated on the sofa.

"He was the only person I ever loved who loved me back," her voice rasped softly, an accusatory tone hunching the words. Sarah Rogan's withered face otherwise had no expression; her dark eyes, glistening with moisture, stared blankly at the dying embers in the fireplace.

Horace Rogan stood with one hand on the ornately wrought brass door handle. He had been ready to leave following his noon meal for the rest of his day at the bank. Sarah had been inconsolable when she first heard the news that Obbie had been killed — from Noah Pine, not from her husband — and the sadness and sense of loss had weighted her life into a long, sustained silence broken now only by occasional outbursts of sobbing. This was the first time she had spoken to her husband since the accident.

"There was nothing I could do," Rogan said, turning back into the room and glancing at Sarah's huddled form on the sofa, a handkerchief clasped tightly into a ball in her right hand. "You know that."

Sarah suddenly came to life and her deep-sunken eyes flashed at him.

"I know that you are almighty glad Obbie's dead. I know that much, Horace!"

"Would you mind keeping your voice down, Sarah? I'm afraid Mrs. Gates has quite enough gossip to pass on about this household without your giving her more. Especially such a baseless remark as that." Rogan sighed audibly. "Obbie turned out bad. That's something you've never been able to admit. I kept him on at the bank more out of charity and my feeling of responsibility for him than because

I ever thought he would make a success in banking."

"And he hated you for it!" Sarah said bitingly, animated now by the wicked relish which had become her way of dealing with her husband.

"I doubt very much that he hated me for keeping him on at the bank," Rogan said, his voice heavy with sarcasm. "But for what I paid him, he couldn't have been gambling and carousing and wenching to all hours of the night."

"Horace Rogan! I will not have you speak of such things under this roof."

"Why? Because you know they're true? Admit it. Obbie was wasting his youth, his life away, carrying on the way he did."

"Ha! That's how wrong you are. Obbie had every intention of leaving the bank, *and leaving you,* just as soon as he made his strike."

"And where was he going to make his 'strike'? At the gaming tables in Hal Owen's Gold Bar Saloon?"

Sarah seemed momentarily flustered. "I don't know where he expected to make his strike, but he told me only two days before he was killed that it wasn't going to be long any more. That he would be leaving this town and you and all he detested behind him."

63

"And what did you say when he told you that?"

"I wished him Godspeed!" Sarah's defiance made her aging face seem oddly skewed, both hating and implacable, as she stared at the man who had fathered her only child.

"Maybe if you had been more supportive of me, we wouldn't have lost Obbie," Horace said. "You always did delight in undermining me and all that I stand for in this town. And don't think that didn't have its way with Obbie. He always knew, no matter how much trouble he got himself into, he could come to you and you would be sympathetic and bail him out." A certain deep, inner triumph now touched Rogan's cheeks under the flare of his temper. "Until he got himself in the wrong place at the wrong time with that riffraff, Ben Massingale, Sam Crowley, and the others."

"Didn't I tell you, Horace? I said it and it's true. You're glad Obbie's dead."

It seemed as if it took all her spirit to get those words out, and having said them now once more, her body seemed to collapse in upon itself again. She shook her head slowly, almost painfully, and the tears seemed to squeeze from out of her eyes.

Rogan's anger left him as swiftly as it had erupted. He knew better than to reach out to this woman, to try and assuage her pain.

He brushed back the quick rush of compassion he felt well up inside him. No good could come from it. As he reflected on it, no good had come from the marriage he had made with this woman. She had become a stranger to him and, he supposed, it was the same with her. Without saying more, Horace turned and let himself out of the parlor and then walked quickly across the foyer and out the front door.

The sun burned bright and hot as soon as Rogan's figure emerged from beneath the protective limbs of the trees shading the house. The wind was blowing hard and had a definite snap to it. The banker pulled his hat down firmly, shading his eyes, as he walked along the path that led to the main street. There was one stop he had to make before he returned to the bank.

Rogan found Acting Marshal Isom Rastrow sitting behind the desk that only a few days ago had belonged to Noah Pine. Rastrow was reading an old newspaper he had found somewhere and chewing heartily at a plug of tobacco. The addition of a porcelain cuspidor beside the desk was the one addition he had made to the room since Silas Pine had been there, dozing and waiting for Noah and the posse to return the day of the robbery. Hearing the banker enter the office, Rastrow put aside the newspaper and accurately sent a stream of spittle into the cuspidor.

Rogan seemed to disapprove of the lawman's presence.

"Don't tell me you've served those eviction notices already on the Massingale and Crowley places."

"Nope," said Rastrow, a tight smile breaking through the days' old stubble around his mouth, his teeth showing yellow and jagged. "I reckon it's been taken care o' though. I sent Acting Deputies Poteet and Banes to the Massingale place and Ellis and Price out to Crowley's."

"I don't like that," Rogan said, his voice touched by agitation. "I'd prefer you were with them. What if Ben Massingale were to show up while Poteet and Banes are out there?"

"Then he'll get himself plugged, just like he's going to get when we find him. I figure it'd be all the easier if he came down from the mountains and got it now, before we have to go up there huntin' him."

"I think you're underestimating Massingale," Rogan said, his mood at once stern and worried. "He shot and killed Noah Pine, didn't he?"

"Sure, from ambush."

"Well, what's to prevent him from having his place staked out, figuring some of the posse might come looking for him."

Rastrow's grin, if anything, was broader than before as he cynically studied the banker. "If he's got his place staked out, Rogan, you can bet it's because he knows you intend to foreclose, not because he thinks some of the posse might be sniffin' around for him."

"I doubt that foreclosure was foremost in his mind when he and the others held up the bank."

"Now, there, Mr. Rogan I opin' I disagree. I think that foreclosure was what brought them to try and pull that job in the first place."

"Perhaps you're right," the banker conceded, distracted now and walking nervously toward the window to look out onto the windswept main street. "Maybe I pushed him and Crowley and the others too hard."

"Well, someone shore pushed 'em," Rastrow said. "They warn't preepared nohow to pull off that job. Hell, we mowed two of 'em down right in the street and loot they got was a dummy, warn't it?"

"The loot, as you refer to it, happens to be money that belongs to the bank's depositors. We had every right to protect it."

"Shore thing, Mr. Rogan. And we helped

67

you save that money for them depositors, didn't we?"

"I know you did, Isom," the banker said, turning toward Rastrow and trying to make his voice sound more cordial than he felt. "And, once we get those foreclosures completed, you'll have the horse ranch you've wanted, a whole section. Also, lest you forget, it is the bank that is paying the salary of your special deputies until Massingale is apprehended."

"Oh, he'll find hisself caught all right, if that old coot pa of the marshal's don't get in the way of my men doing what they know best how to do. Trackin' an outlaw horse or an outlaw, it's all the same to them, and they're good at it."

"At this point I'd be satisfied if they just manage to get those women and their families started away from their places and away from here."

"Think Massingale is likely to follow that woman and girl of his, if they do lite out?"

"I'm sure of it."

And you don't care if he does, Rastrow thought to himself. He knew this about Horace Rogan without being at all certain just what it meant, or how it was Rogan had known Massingale and the others had been planning to hit the bank. In fact, there were a lot of things Rastrow didn't know, but he did know what he had told his men and he didn't figure either Massingale's fetching wife or his daughter would be in a mood to do much traveling that day. Once their work was done, let Massingale return. They'd be ready for him. Horace Rogan's voice broke in on his musing.

"What?"

"I said, I have to get back to the bank."

Rastrow was almost apologetic as he approached the older man.

"I 'spect everything will turn out just as you want it to, Mr. Rogan."

"Report to me after your deputies get back to town."

"You can bank on it, Mr. Rogan," Rastrow said slyly, and was surprised when Rogan didn't seem the least amused.

The banker silently left the marshal's office, again pulling firmly on his hat as he felt once more the harsh wind blowing down from the Neversummers, tinged now with a colder bite than it had had when he'd left his home earlier.

Chapter Seven

It was nearly a minute before Shawn Massingale pushed open the door a few cautious inches and then stepped out. She was carrying her rifle two-handed and was obviously prepared for anything, since she couldn't be sure of Silas Pine's part in any of this.

"Over here," Pine called.

Shawn advanced slowly across the short clearing till she had a plain view of both of them and could take in the situation at a glance. Her face was almost calm, but a man could sense the hatred boiling behind it as she stared at Poteet.

"It appears ye've saved my bacon, Mr. Pine," she murmured between her teeth.

"Could be. Your daughter, now. . . ."

"Where is she?"

"She's fine. That Banes man must of tormented her a bit, but he's dead as a man can be. I seen to that."

"I asked ye where she is."

"Around back of your cabin where I left her. She calms down a mite, reckon she can tell you all of what happened. Then come

70

back here, if you will. I'll hold onto this one."

Without a word Shawn turned and ran back around the cabin, crying, "Kerry Lu! Kerry Lu!"

"I didn't do nothing to that girl," Poteet said surlily.

"So you said. But you'd maybe have done it yourself, later on," Pine added relentlessly. "And maybe to her ma, too, if you'd got her alive."

"Hey now," Poteet said in an angry voice, "I. . . ."

"Shut your mouth. All I want to know right now is what you prime specimens was setting to do here?"

Poteet shifted slightly so that the deputy marshal's badge pinned to his shirt beneath the cowhide vest was more clearly visible.

"Banes and I are here on marshal's office business."

"And what business might that be?" Silas asked, his mind not quite sure how to take this turn of events. But then, someone would have to replace Noah. But Rastrow and his hardcases? It didn't make sense.

"I've got eviction notices in my inside vest pocket here, signed by Judge Llewellyn Y. Tabor, and Marshal Rastrow asked us to serve them on Massingale. Ellis and Price is servin' a similar notice at the Crowley place. We are to see that the Massingales pack up and move out. After that, we're going to set up a watch at this here Massingale place and wait for her old man to try and slip back. You've heard, haven't you, that Horace Rogan has put a price on that bastard's scalp? A thousand dollars, cold cash. We could use the money. And in the meantime, we've been appointed special deputies and are drawing wages."

"I've heard nothing," Pine said coldly. "I been stalking this place for a week, staying close by. Massingale ain't here. Ain't been here."

Poteet whistled gently. "Well, maybe watchin' this place will be a waste of time, then. I know you got reason to fetch Massingale. Maybe a better one than us or Mr. Rogan."

"Maybe."

"Look, Mr. Pine. Why stay on the peck with us? We're honest, sworn-in, official deputies doin' the law's work here. Massingale's a fugitive. Marshal Rastrow and the deputy sheriff from over at Glade where that Injun 'breed just discovered gold have both been sending search parties out in the mountains. They ain't come up with nothin' neither. But you. . . . You're staking everything on that Massingale will show back here. Ain't that it?"

"Maybe he will, maybe he won't."

Poteet drew up his shoulders. "You ain't telling much."

"I don't need to. You're on the wrong side of my piece. You just answer up when I ask."

"Sure, Mr. Pine. But I gotta suggestion."

"Spit it out."

"How 'bout you throwin' in with Isom and us? You're a prime man on trackin'. I know that. You could maybe turn up something where them town counterjumpers goin' out in posses can't."

Pine eyed the man with a fathomless contempt. "Now that Banes is out of it?"

"Bruno always took his own chances. So did we. Man, we partnered up, but there wa'n't no love lost betwixt us. There'll still be a five-way split on old Rogan's bounty, that's if. . . ."

"Shut up," Pine rasped warningly. "I don't hanker to hear any more out of you. I'd sooner pair with a pack of skunk-bit coyotes. I'll leave Miz Massingale to tell her side of this."

They waited in silence.

When Shawn Massingale returned, her face was almost empty. But both her hands were still gripped around the rifle.

"She's all right. Me lass's all right. But that filthy brute got his hands on her before she broke away and ran."

73

"No matter now, ma'am. He's done."

"But this blackg'ard's still alive." She pushed a straggle of red hair back from her temple and stared at Poteet, the fury radiating from her eyes.

"Miz Massingale, now simmer down. Don't try something you'll come to regret."

"I won't. And I sure as hell wouldn't regret it, Mr. Pine. Na ever. Ye can lay odds to that."

Pine would, too. She had more fire combined with an icy determination than he'd ever seen in one woman. But she had good sense and a steely self-discipline about her, and she held still now.

"How did this fracas get started, ma'am?"

"I was out hanging up me wash. Those two spalpeen rode in and demanded to search our place for me husband. They also said they had a paper from the bank saying we had to get out. They'd search first and then we were to put what we could in our wagon and leave. That's when I run inside and grabbed up me rifle and shot at 'em. They laid up out here and shot back. Then I saw that Kerry Lu was gone. She'd been outside playing, I wasna sure where. Afterwards I realized that there was only one man firing and that one — Banes, ye called him — was missing. I figured he might be after Kerry Lu . . . but there was naething I could do. Na a thing!"

74

Pine exhaled a long breath. "Glad you had the sense not to try. You, now," he said, motioning his weapon at Poteet, "you get the hell out of here. Get your horse and go bury your fat chum if you want. He's out back of the ridge yonder. Then get the hell out of here. Don't come back. I catch sight of you, or Rastrow, or any more of your gang, I'll kill you on sight."

Poteet reacted sharply, his voice wheezy and querulous. "What about this woman and her kid gettin' off this place? You goin' up against the law?"

"You're goddamned right I am."

"What about my rifle?"

"Replace it when you get the time. But for right now, shuck that pistol belt too . . . yeah, right here. *Then get moving.*"

Poteet was gone. In a stony, even forbidding manner, Shawn Massingale invited Pine to the cabin for a cup of coffee. A little warily he seated himself at the trestle table, carefully noting that she laid the rifle well aside before she began to grind the coffee beans. He was aware of intermittent shuttling glances of mingled hostility and bemused puzzlement flashing toward him.

He could guess at what she was thinking. Finally he cleared his throat. "Miz Massingale, you're wondering what I was doing here-abouts."

"Nae need to wonder," she said tartly. "Ye came looking for me man to show up. I reckon it was lucky for us, Kerry Lu and me, that ye'd shewn up when ye did. Lord knows, we're owing ye for that."

She don't know I been watching the cabin all along, Pine thought in relief. It would be senseless to continue his vigil if she were aware of what he was doing.

But then, maybe she was. He couldn't be sure. Massingale might even have drifted in and out clandestinely during a nightly inter-lude when Pine had been asleep. . . .

"I'm sorry about y'r lad," she said flatly, almost tonelessly. "But ye were looking to kill Ben. Ye opened fire first on Sam and him. Al Ferguson was one o' your possemen. He dropped by later and told me."

"That's right," he said wearily, rasping a hand over his untrimmed beard. "But if they hadn't been running away, they wouldn't have got tracked down. Or shot at."

She poured a cup of steaming brew and brought it over and lightly slammed it down on the table in front of him. "They figured what they stole was due 'em. So do I when I think about it."

"Yeah," Pine said sourly. "You would."

"And ye don't!"

"Don't know nothing about it, 'cept my son's dead, ma'am."

Shawn set her fists squarely on her hips in what, by now, he could recognize as an habitual gesture of mulish defiance. "What do ye ken of *justice*, Mr. Pine?"

"Where I'm from, I'm mostly a lone man," Pine observed wryly. "We don't much define things like justice. You do what you think you got to do to stay alive. That's enough. I . . . hadn't seen my boy Noah in a long time and when I rode into Grafton I had a chance to help track Crowley and your husband. No more to it."

"Wasn't there?"

She folded her arms and turned away, her mouth tautly set.

Kerry Lu came in from the sleeping area and halted in the doorway. She was fully dressed in a well-worn gingham dress and high-topped shoes and her young face looked darkly sober.

But she gazed squarely at Pine and said quietly, not a tremor in her voice, "I guess I owe you my life, sir."

Maybe you owe me a sight more than you know, Pine thought, but only nodded politely, raised his cup in mild salute and sipped more of the scalding brew. It was damned good coffee.

Kerry Lu's glance sifted away from him now; maybe she was uneasily mindful of how he had seen her nearly naked. She was plainly a modest girl, no doubt trained that way by her mother.

"That other man is gone now, Miss Kerry," he said gently. "I don't reckon he'll be back. That one I got sure won't."

"Ye can bet they'll be back," Shawn said hotly, bluntly. "They want us off this place, don't they? Horace Rogan wants us off this place and sooner or later he'll drive us off. Now, damn it, Mr. Pine, why can't ye just leave us alone and not add to our miseries? All right . . . me man shot your son. Maybe. Fergy told me everyone thought so. But Lord, isn't that enough bloodshed? Why keep hounding us?"

"That ain't my aim," Pine said doggedly. "I want to take your husband alive. . . ."

"But if ye can't, ye'll take him dead! That's all you're living for now, isn't it? Isn't it, Mr. Pine?"

Silas Pine swigged down what remained of his coffee, draining the cup. He set it down and picked up his rifle and swung off the trestle table bench. He walked to the door, swung it open and closed it behind him, never looking back and saying nothing.

Chapter Eight

It was somewhat before the time when she usually got up, but Susan Gates couldn't think of any good reason for staying in bed when she couldn't sleep anyway. Aurelia Crowley's baby had been crying on and off all night. The infant was named Hope and mother and child had been staying at the Gates's little house since they buried Sam Crowley's body in the town cemetery. In an off-hand moment, Susan had remarked to Aurelia that Hope seemed an unusual name for a baby girl with dark skin.

"Sho'nuff, it is, Miss Susan, but my man Sam believed dat da West was a second chance fer all of us, white folks *and* black folks. And dat's why he came up with dat name. I still" — her voice trembled now as she spoke — "I . . . still thinks dat's the right name fer our little 'un. Even after what's all happened, I mean to Sam and us and all. Yes'm, Miss Susan, Hope it is and Hope it's goin' to stay."

Susan had doubled up with her mother so Aurelia and Hope could share Susan's room. Helen Gates had liked Aurelia Crowley from the first time they met at Rawina Pine's small trading post where Susan worked afternoons five days a week and all day Saturday for fifteen cents an hour. It was scarcely a fancy wage, but with what her mother made being housekeeper for the Rogans, they were managing quite nicely.

It would have been heartless to abandon Aurelia and Hope to trying to make a go of it at the Crowley place with Sam gone. She and the baby were better off in town. At least her mother's surmise had seemed right at the time. But Hope somehow seemed profoundly anguished. Helen had feared that perhaps there was something wrong with Hope inside. That's why they had sent word to Doctor Whitelaws. It had taken the medico several hours to respond because he also served as coroner for the district and had been summoned to a nearby ranch where a man had had his neck broken mounting a jittery horse. But there was nothing wrong internally with Hope. Probably it was the times, Doc had suggested, and there had been time aplenty lately for death and for dying, Susan reflected morbidly to herself as she went about lighting the kitchen stove. She then went outside to fetch water for the tea kettle and other morning chores.

The light was only a dull gray; it was windy.

Susan's calico dress clung to her and she couldn't help shivering.

Aurelia Crowley was in the kitchen by the time Susan returned.

"She's done finally got down fer de night, I think," Aurelia said, and smiled wanly. "We sho'nuff is an extra chore fer you folks, and mebbe it's time now we was gettin' back to our place."

"Ma wouldn't hear of it," Susan said simply, walking to the sink carrying the wooden water bucket, "and I won't either. Now what would you be doing out at your place, you with a baby to care for and no one to fetch for you?"

"All de same," Aurelia went on, her eyes following Susan's movements, "Ah think it can't help but prey on yo' mind now an' agin, that my Sam was part of de reason your Noah got himself killed."

Susan stopped what she was doing and turned to the other woman, leaning back against the wooden cabinet housing the stone sink.

"I'll hear none of that kind of talk. They say it was Ben Massingale who did for Noah Pine, and no one else. Noah's ma blames his pa for what happened. If Noah and the posse hadn't been using him as a tracker, they maybe wouldn't have blundered onto the place where Ben and Sam were camped."

81

"Ah don't see howsome she can blame dat old man."

"She does, though. He deserted her once, her and Noah, long ago and went to live with some Indian woman, a Navajo I hear, from that group camped up above Glade. Silas Pine was no good, not ever, according to Rawina, and his tagging along with Noah and that posse was just asking for trouble. I would sooner agree with her and blame old Pine for Noah's death than your Sam who didn't live long enough to fire a shot at anyone."

There were tears in Susan's eyes. Perhaps the mood was catching. Aurelia felt tears coming to her eyes too.

"And," Susan said, speaking rapidly, "do you know what happened at Noah's funeral? Silas Pine was there. Rawina said I should cut him off cold if he came over to speak to me. But, big-hearted Susan, I wouldn't listen. I went up to him and told him who I was. That Noah and I had been engaged to be married. That we'd not set the date but we loved each other deeply."

"What did he say when you told him dat?"

"Not so much as a howdy-do. He just motioned at me as if I were some stranger blocking his way and pushed on past where I was standing. I was so angry I 'low I would've screamed if ma and Rawina had not come up then. 'The man is a swine,' Rawina said. 'I told you not to speak to him. You wouldn't listen. That's how Silas Pine treats everyone. Everyone except himself.' And," Susan's voice dropped to a hush, "and maybe Noah. Oh, I remember that the night in town after the robbery, when the men had come back and before they were going out again when it got light. Noah had supper that night with his pa. He came over here afterwards to see me. He seemed pleased somehow, that he was finally able to get along with his father. Silas had hurt him so when he deserted them. Noah would never get over it, I thought. He didn't even like to talk about his father except to say he wished he'd stay good and far away and not bother him any more."

"It don't speak well fer dat man. Ah'm thinkin' he'll have a lot to answer fer when de day of judgment comes fer him."

"I reckon he will," Susan said sharply, clipping it off there and turning to the tea kettle, taking it over to the stove.

"Ma'll be up soon, Aurelia. I got some really fine jasmine tea yesterday from Rawina. It just came in a shipment all the way from San Francisco, she said. If it tastes half as good as it smells, ma'll be sure to love it."

"You all are managin' to get by jes' fine, you, your ma, and Missus Pine. Sometimes

83

Ah think dere's no reason in God's earth dat Ah couldn't make a go of it out at de place once Hope is over her miseries. We could sort of comfort each other, now and again, an' when she's older she could help out."

Susan was lifting down the china teapot from its place of honor on the crockery shelf.

"I didn't want to mention it," she said, "but there's talk around the trading post that the bank is calling in the notes on the places of all the men who were involved in that robbery."

To Susan's surprise, Aurelia laughed.

"Ah 'spect dey'll have more'n a little trouble with Shawn Massingale when it comes to somethin' like dat. She didn't trust dat Obbie Rogan any more than Ah did and she done tol' Ben so at the time, and told him loud, way Ben tells it."

"Best not say anything more about what happened," Helen Gates said, bustling hurriedly into the room. She had the same clear blue eyes Susan did, the same high cheekbones, the same straight nose, but there the resemblance ended. Her blonde hair was more than a little touched with pale white strands and her figure was more buxom. "It would kill Miz Rogan if she ever heard anything bad whatsoever about Obbie."

"She'll have to find out eventually, won't

she, Ma?" Susan asked.

"Reckon not, Susie. Who's even going to bring up the matter any more now that Horace Rogan has himself a marshal more to his liking?"

"Dat Isom Rastrow is white trash from de back hills of Kaintuck'. Ah know de type all too well. Ah figger he's de one dat did fer my Sam."

"Possibly," Helen said as she brought down three teacups and three saucers for what had by now become a morning ritual for these three. She had no intention of telling Aurelia that she had met Rastrow on the street the day before when she was on her way home. He had stopped to let her know that he and a lot of other white folks around these parts didn't appreciate no nigger staying in town. Mrs. Crowley's place was back at her shack packing up her possibles and heading out of the district. In fact, he had sent a couple of deputies out to the Crowley place that day to evict her, and then what should he see, but her prancing along the street in town with that squalling baby of hers.

Helen had told him to his face, that if he didn't like it, that was just too bad. Aurelia and Hope were staying with them for as long as was needed. She also said she intended to bring up the eviction matter with Mr. Rogan as soon as she saw him the next day. That had taken Rastrow aback some. He had given her a puzzled, almost helpless look, it seemed to her at the time and had gone on his way.

As the three women chatted pleasantly over their tea, Helen Gates became more resolved than before on what she would do. Obbie Rogan, she had learned, was as much responsible for what had happened at the bank as Sam Crowley or any of the other small ranchers. It was time someone reminded Obbie's father of that and put a stop to whatever it was he had in mind. If she was right in her surmise, he wouldn't want anyone to know the truth about Obbie, but not because he wanted to protect Sarah. Obbie had been shot during that robbery and, according to Aurelia, not by any of the men who had tried to hold up the bank.

Chapter Nine

Pine wasn't really sure what to do next. Shawn Massingale was now definitely aware that he was waiting for a chance to seize her husband should he return to their cabin. Or, possibly, shoot him down if there was no other way to get him.

Also, Silas was beginning to feel more unsure of his own motives. So far he had been driven only by consideration of Noah's dying. But now he was questioning himself about that. Maybe it was inevitable. Maybe as time passed, the original reason would become less pressing . . . less real.

Wavering between uncertainties, Pine took up his usual vigil that evening. He dozed off heavily a couple of times and bitterly realized that he was in damned sorry condition for keeping up this kind of round-the-clock watch much longer.

But tonight he fell into a jackpot of luck, although he didn't recognize it as such right off.

Once more dozing on his haunches on the height above the Massingale place, as twilight turned to a velvet darkness, Pine jerked suddenly erect. There was a light. It was moving slowly back and forth across the rear window of the cabin. A lamp was being swung slowly to and fro, held by someone inside.

Fully alert now, Pine shrank down more tightly among the rocks, just enough so that his eyes could see over the tops. A signal of some kind was being given to someone outside. That's what it had to be . . . but a signal for what?

Suddenly he understood.

Her husband was out there, watching the place, and this was her way of telling him it wasn't safe for him to come in. That was it, then. Massingale and his wife had prearranged everything between them sometime back. In fact, Massingale might well have paid a call or two here at a time when Pine had been sleeping or had been off guard.

And now Shawn knew he was watching the cabin and why. That left Pine with only one option if he was to capture Ben Massingale. No matter how weary he might feel, he would set out tomorrow.

Silas Pine climbed into the saddle after — for once — a good long sleep, but he had still felt dog-tired when he roused himself. It was nearly mid-morning by now, but the sky was gray and overcast, no spark of true daylight to it, and the wind had a cold, damp bite to it. All in all the weather was a pretty fair match for his mood.

Pine had thrown his gear together with savagely jerky motions, had diamond-hitched it onto his pack horse, and had mounted up. Now, as he swung out of the clearing, he did not look back, only forward. As he passed by it, a heavy mound of turned earth a little off to his right among the trees did not escape his notice. Poteet had obviously buried Bruno Banes where he'd fallen.

And he'd meet Rastrow and Poteet and the others up there somewhere, he thought, turning his gaze toward the backing heights. They hadn't gotten in their execution yet. Not of Massingale. And their chance for the reward Rogan had posted. That probably would now come before getting either the Massingale women or the Crowleys off their places. And this time their eyes would be peeled for Silas Pine, too.

It occurred to him to cut off at an angle in order to reach the spot from which Massingale might have been watching his place last night and would have been turned away by his wife's signal. Massingale was a cunning woodsman, he would grant him that. Thus far, according to Poteet, he'd successfully eluded the posses out searching for him. Rastrow and Poteet and that horse-hunting crew were no strangers to the wilds, either. And they had been with some of the groups.

When he reached what he felt was the most likely spot, Pine dismounted and ground-hitched his horse. He paced a wide circle, working inward, giving the ground beneath him an intent scrutiny. Massingale would have approached his place with great stealth, enough to throw off easily any ordinary man looking for track.

Finally Pine came upon something definite. A scuffed deep-dug heelprint on a miniature patch of bare soil. He dropped to one knee beside it, carefully studying it, then slowly scanned the ground roundabout.

Nothing else. That was all. Massingale must have turned quickly away after seeing the signal light, unaware of this one slip-up. Then he would have faded away into the dark-shrouded heights. . . .

God damn!

Pine got up and worked outward again, scrutinizing the mixture of prairie grass and wild shrubbery and few traces of naked earth with a savage intensity. It was useless. There was no more sign to be found. Massingale had gotten clean away, leaving nothing by which to track him. Pine stood scowling as he scraped

90

a hand over the harsh bristle of his beard.

All right. Then he'd have to start all over. From scratch.

In a way, the idea wasn't altogether an unwelcome one. It might take a lot of time finally to run down Ben Massingale. On the other hand, Pine thought pessimistically, what else did he have to do with the rest of his own life . . . *after Noah?*

He worked slowly upward into the higher country, keeping his senses attuned to a sharp edge. He might run unexpectedly into Massingale or even Rastrow and his crew. He cared nothing about that except for encountering them accidentally.

Maybe, he thought dully, he wouldn't really mind if they did get to Massingale ahead of him. It would relieve him of the responsibility of having to shoot the man down if he refused to surrender.

But so far Rastrow and the others hadn't shown any sign of being able to catch up with Massingale. Maybe Rastrow had suspected that Massingale was watching his place and for that reason he had sent Poteet and Banes to evict his family. To remove Shawn as a possible source of aid to her husband. Or maybe to get Massingale angry enough, or worried enough, to come in to see if he could meet up with Shawn and Kerry Lu without the advantage of any signals.

Pine brushed all such speculation aside. *I can't quit,* he kept thinking obsessively, doggedly. *I can't quit.*

So he concentrated on scanning the ground with renewed care, even climbing down now and then to check more closely for possible track.

The terrain was highly varied. It changed from heavy brush to forested areas to long stretches of open and lumpy prairie. Pine was working across it sort of aimlessly, as he had no track to follow. But he held to a more or less southerly direction, keeping his bearings locked to the westward swing of the sun. Always, especially on the open places, he fought hard to keep his sluggish and weary senses particularly alert for almost anything.

It would be too damned easy to get himself potted by a sniper concealed in any nearby cover.

When the sun finally slid down behind tall peaks to the west, bringing an early darkness, Pine had to acknowledge to himself that he was about done in. He went through the mechanical motions of dismounting in a clearing thickly surrounded by trees, watering the horses at a nearby spring that slowly bubbled up from below and hobbling them out on a patch of grass. Afterward he built a small fire and cooked up a little grub and some coffee.

Somehow everything that had happened since he hit Grafton had conspired to make him put out of his mind what before then had been so urgent. His own deteriorating physical condition. The post doctor had counseled him to avoid exercise and excitement, and what had he been doing ever since his arrival? He was living just as he always lived when on a hunt. It was entirely possible that he wouldn't be alive much longer. In fact, to hear that doctor tell it, it was a certainty.

He had finished eating, his mind running over the diagnosis of his heart condition, when some obscure sixth sense — he had felt it other times and wasn't at all sure how to describe it — roused him to a conviction that something was lurking nearby. His blaze, although tiny and almost smokeless, might have attracted whatever it was.

But was it a man or an animal?

He'd bet it was human. An animal would have made at least a small betraying sound. A really knowledgeable woodsman wouldn't.

Pine, crouched by the fire, knew he was a plain target for an armed man. Or would be shortly, if the intruder worked in any nearer.

Yawning, he got slowly and achingly to his

feet and stretched his arms, then held his hands out toward the fire, as if casually to warm them. He wanted to appear absolutely at ease and unsuspecting for the moment.

When nothing happened, he went swiftly about his next moves. He piled a heap of his gear to about the length of a man's body near the fire and flung his blankets over it so that it simulated the form of a sleeping man with the blankets drawn over his head. The wind was still sharp and chilled enough to make that seem natural.

Then he picked up his rifle and loped quickly and silently into a flank of the surrounding trees and sank down on his haunches at a spot where he could readily command a good view of his campfire.

Pine waited long and with increasing discomfort for what seemed endless minutes. Actually the time was much shorter, as he knew, but tired as he was and as acutely aware of a probable danger, he was able to fight back any encroaching drowsiness. But he could not prevent his body from growing increasingly cold and stiff with the night's increasing chill, although here at least he was out of the wind. It was getting harder all the time to be poised enough to respond when, finally, the watcher made his move.

It must have taken him all this time to work

in so close. Pine saw a faint stirring among the trees beyond, and then a man came into view, making no sound at all. He was carrying a rifle, and he stepped quickly around the dying fire and over to the blanket-covered pile.

He nudged the blankets partly aside with his rifle barrel, then straightened up with a startled grunt, as he made out in the dim illumination from the fire what was underneath.

"You can freeze right there," Pine said in a cold, clear voice. "I've got a bead square on your head. Ben Massingale, ain't it?"

Chapter Ten

Directly upon hearing from Reno Poteet what had happened at the Massingale place, Isom Rastrow had sworn out a warrant charging Silas Pine with murder, obstruction of justice, and resisting arrest. Although he seemed to Rastrow somewhat reluctant to do it, old Judge Llewellyn Tabor signed the warrant for Silas Pine's arrest on the charges stated.

The loss of Bruno Banes left Rastrow more dependent on Black Ellis and Lefty Price. Ellis had blunt features, small, obsidian eyes for which he was probably named, and carried a surprising bulk for a man who made his living horse hunting in the valleys of the Neversummers. Lefty Price was squat, compact, and when he took his hat off had a head almost entirely bald except for a small tuft of hair that rose up in the very center of his head like a Pawnee scalp lock.

Rastrow knew now Aurelia Crowley was not at her place but here in town staying with the Gates women. He called a meeting with Ellis, Price, and Poteet just as soon as they were all back and told them what had to be done now. The next morning, Rastrow formed another search posse from among the men who had first been out after Massingale and Crowley, the blacksmith, the saloon bouncer, the shopkeeper, and in place of the two teamsters who had since left town he added a couple of drifters that Hal Owen brought along from his Gold Bar Saloon.

Aurelia Crowley heard the wagon pull around the side of the house just as she managed to get Hope down after more than an hour's nursing. It had been another bad night. She was more convinced than ever that if Hope's disposition did not improve, no matter what Helen and Susan Gates said, she would go back to the dirt ranch Sam and she had homesteaded even if she might lose it any time now. The knock at the back door was so loud, she rushed to answer it, afraid that Hope would surely waken if it was repeated.

"Miz Crowley?" the man in the forefront asked.

"Yes?" She could smell the liquor on his breath but she also saw the star pinned to his cowhide vest.

"I'm Acting Deputy Marshal Poteet and this man with me is another special deputy helping us out at the marshal's office."

"What is it you want?" Aurelia asked in

a hushed tone. "I have a. . ."

"If you'll step back inside the house, we'll get to our reason for bein' here," Poteet said. He pushed his way in through the open door, Black Ellis right behind him.

"What is it you want?" Aurelia repeated, her voice rising slightly in hesitation and fear.

"We've got a few questions we'd like to ask," Poteet said as Ellis closed the outside door and stood with his back against it. "About that gossip you been spreading around on how those bank robbers didn't shoot down Obbie Rogan."

Aurelia's right hand went toward her mouth as she took in air quickly. It was as far as she got. All in a motion, Poteet's hand flashed up with his Colt, bringing it around quickly and suddenly against the side of her head. She let out a short moan and slid to the floor. Holstering his gun, Poteet turned to Ellis who had moved into the kitchen for a closer look.

"Get Lefty in here with that tarpaulin," Poteet said. "We've got no time to spare. Isom should be just about pulling out by now."

Before Silas Pine rode out that morning, Shawn Massingale had been watching him as he packed up his camp. She was dressed in corduroy trousers, a red plaid shirt (an old one of Ben's), riding boots, and a light-colored peaked sombrero with three triangular creases. The boots were old but the leather was soft and comfortable. About her neck she wore a blue bandanna. She knew Ben didn't like her to wear pants and had once before threatened to take a harness strap to her backside if she wore them again. But that couldn't be helped now, with what lay before her. At her side she had a worn leather holster and an 1872 .32-20 Colt with a six-inch barrel which Ben had taught her to shoot. What spare ammunition she had conserved was carried in the cylindrical loops of the gunbelt strapped around her narrow waist and it supported the holster held fast by a flap of leather attached at the top and bottom.

Once Pine's figure disappeared into the distance, Shawn made her way swiftly back to the cabin. Her signal last night had surely warned Ben off. They had set up that signal just before he pulled out the night of the attempted robbery. He had managed to see her twice since, once when the posse was in pursuit and once more recently.

She had stuck it out during this time because of the obligation she felt in having agreed to operate a stage station at which twice a day coaches would pull in for a change of horses. All along she had been regularly providing food and coffee for the passengers, but she gave that up day before yesterday using as her reason Ben's being a fugitive and it no longer mattered to her. Today she was willing to abandon the horses, and even the cabin. She wasn't fooled in the least by what had happened when Banes and Poteet had shown up intent on evicting her. Banes was dead, buried out back, and Poteet was certain to come again with a force sufficient to move her off the land.

Besides, what did it all come to now? Silas Pine intended either to capture Ben or to kill him in the attempt. There were posses out searching for Ben. It would only be a question of time. If she could do it, Shawn was going to join him. They could ride far and stay in hiding for a while. Later, eventually, they could send for Kerry Lu.

Just what to do about Kerry Lu had really been the only consideration holding her back until now. She didn't dare leave her alone in the cabin. What had happened the other day with Bruno Banes could happen again. And next time she might not be able to ward off danger. Silas Pine had ridden off, probably to go about his dark plan.

She had thought at first that she might take Kerry Lu over to the Crowley place where she could put up for a spell with Aurelia and Baby Hope. But she would be no better protected there than she was here. Under other circumstances Shawn might have asked Rawina Pine to take in Kerry Lu. They had been friendly since the Massingales had settled in the district and Shawn had often made her town purchases at Rawina's trading post. But with Ben accused of having killed Rawina's son and with Rawina's former husband tracking down Ben, that was no answer either. She would have liked to have unloaded on Pine that it wasn't Ben's bullet that had killed his son, but how could she without letting on that they had been in contact? Now that old fool was on his trail again. Besides, even if she had admitted having seen Ben and had said he denied shooting Noah, would Silas Pine have believed her? Shawn doubted it.

By a painful process of elimination she had finally decided on Santiago Cruz, a cousin of Diego Cruz's, the old and admired horse-breaker at the great Swallowtail ranch. Santiago was some years younger than Diego and not nearly so skilled with horses. He worked as a hostler at the livery stable in Grafton and his wife, Mariana, was proficient at weaving rugs with Navajo designs. As far as Shawn knew, Mariana was herself part Navajo.

Ben used frequently to go hunting with Gage Cameron, a half-breed who had struck it rich some months back and now had moved up in the world. In leaner times for the Camerons, Gage had once taken all three of the Massingales with him to visit the camp of old Adakhai. The Navajo shaman and his people lived in relative peace and isolation from the white settlements which circled them. She had liked old Adakhai and his people, but their acquaintance was limited to that one visit. Santiago Cruz had stopped by on his way back from Swallowtail where he had gone to visit his cousin Diego. It was Santiago who had read Shawn's mind so accurately that she almost jumped off the floor when he suggested that he and Mariana could take in Kerry Lu if Shawn was of a mind to be with her man.

"There are many places to hide in the Neversummers," he had said in his soft voice, and his gentle dark eyes seemed filled with a pain more ancient than the present trouble. "You could always go to Gage. He would help you, no? Gage, he likes Benito, and he likes you. I am escertain he would help."

Shawn had thought about it long and hard. Now her mind was made up. All she had been waiting for was that moment when Silas Pine gave up his watch. Last night her signaling to Ben must have been seen by the old trapper. He knew better now than to sit around in the hope that Ben would let himself be caught returning to visit his family.

Kerry Lu wore a plain dress Shawn had

made special for the occasion. She had it tied up at the calves so she could sit a horse. Ben always said his women were not ever to ride astride, but Ben wasn't around and his objection didn't meet with present necessity. The belongings Kerry Lu was able to fit into an old burlap sack now hung from the horn on the old Spanish saddle on Molly, the Massingale mule she would be riding. Shawn had saddled her roan mare whom she had named Chooky. In addition to her bed roll tied down behind, she had added a second bundle containing a sheepskin coat and what medical supplies she could muster, all neatly rolled into her Navajo rug. That rug she would never leave behind. One last check of the corral to see that the fresh team was fed and watered for later in the day when the stage would pull in, and she was ready.

Shawn mounted and, with Kerry Lu at her side, the two rode out to the main stage road which ran close to the cabin. They had made it into the first clump of tall pines which marked either side of the road as it lifted to a rise when, ahead of them but still out of sight, Shawn heard the sounds of many horses being ridden at a moderately fast pace. Not horses pulling a stage. But horses bunched as in a posse.

Chapter Eleven

Santiago Cruz was a man no longer young. When he walked, he favored his stiff right leg which was a memento of his horse-breaking days. Why, he told himself, if it were not for that unfortunate accident, he might have been as his cousin, Diego Cruz, the great *jinete* of horsemen in the Grafton district. But he himself did not really believe it. No matter how *muy hombre* a man might be around horses, there was when it came to rough-busting those wild *ladinos* one quality a man needed more than any other, a suppleness of the bones. After twenty-five, Diego would say, a man is no good any more for rough-busting. But Santiago seemed to have been born with brittle bones and had been only twenty-one when he had broken his leg, being slammed against a corral post by the *ladino* he was trying to break.

A slight and wiry man, with the years Santiago's face had become wattled with deep grooves that had baked to a brown the color of the leather trousers he wore. His hair was iron-gray but not his drooping mustache

104

which was singularly white, setting off the natural darkness of his face and his pale brown eyes which were as quick and as youthful as those of fourteen-year-old Tip Maginnis. The son of Roy Maginnis, the local blacksmith and a former Army farrier, Tip had helped out around the Grafton Livery Stable and Feed Barn all summer and next week, when school resumed, he wanted to work late afternoons and weekends.

The stable and feed barn belonged to Lew Tabor, the local justice of the peace. There was nothing particularly remarkable in that, but there was about Judge Tabor — as everyone always referred to him. He had spent more than a decade seeking a strike, in the gold fields of California, then amid the Furnace range near Death Valley, in the desert vastness of Nevada and Arizona and near Mormon's Ferry in southwestern Utah. In an accident no less quixotic and unpredictable as that which had given Santiago his stiff leg, the crimping of a dynamite cap had gone awry and Tabor had been blinded at forty years of age.

Even without his sight, the judge had been able to embark on a new career, one as unlikely and freakish as the accident which had befallen him. With the help of an apprentice lawyer in Denver, he had begun the long and painstaking process of reading for the law in the legal firm of Henderson, Pollack, and Harris. He had come to Grafton ten years ago, hung out his shingle, and to the amusement of many in the district specialized in small claims and land patents. He might not be able to see, but he could argue a case in any court better than many and dictate a surprisingly detailed brief. Tabor accomplished these feats in large measure because of the devotion of his daughter, Malinda. She was by now a middle-aged spinster. It was she who continued to read law and case books aloud to her father and who took his dictation in composing briefs, locating citations for him, and maintaining his correspondence. Three years ago there was a vacancy for justice of the peace in the first district and Judge Tabor had run for the office unopposed.

Santiago had only come to Grafton because Mariana wanted to be near her people, those Navajos who had followed the path blazed by old Adakhai and his clan. A few years after the Civil War, the Navajos that had been rounded up in the Canyon de Chelly by Kit Carson and the Union Army to keep them from committing any further depredations that might help the Confederacy in the fight for the Southwest were released and allowed to settle on the new reservation allotted to

106

them. Adakhai had chosen instead to venture north with his clan, all the way to Wyoming.

Mariana considered herself one of *Dineh* even though she lived among the *Belinkanas*. Santiago had first met her when she was being held captive with the other Navajos at the Bosque Redondo along the Pecos River outside Fort Sumner. Adakhai's clan did not wish to ratify the Navajo Treaty of 1868 and settle on the vast reservation set aside for the *Dineh*. He had a vision that the future for his clan was in the new land he sought in a valley of the Neversummers. It was there the clan lived still, more or less in isolation from the white population which was pouring in, filing on homesteads, beginning farms and ranches, or the older established ranches in the area such as the RBJ or the Swallowtail.

It was possibly out of consideration for Santiago, whom she loved deeply and who had gone with her on the trek northward, that Mariana had satisfied herself with a life in town rather than living in a hogan at Adakhai's encampment as her sisters did to this day. Santiago had secured the position of hostler at the livery stable when Grafton had been even more of a one-horse town than it was today. Lew Tabor had bought it from its former owner, who had decided to venture farther West, and Santiago had come along with the deal. He had overseen the expansion of the stable and the building of the feed barn. Judge Tabor trusted him implicitly and even the ever-doting Malinda Tabor permitted Santiago to come to the front door of their cottage when he had business to discuss with the judge rather than going to the rear as did the tradesmen.

It had been shortly after dawn that morning when Black Ellis had come to the stable and ordered Santiago to hitch up a team to a deep-bed wagon that the marshal's office would be renting.

"And what beesness could that bee, *Señor* Ellis?" Santiago had asked in a friendly, conversational manner.

"None of yours, Mex," Ellis had snapped. "Just get a move on."

It was young Tip Maginnis who was helping Santiago with the harnessing who suggested the wagon might be to transport Miz Shawn and Kerry Lu to town.

"She weel not leave without a fight, *muchacho*," Santiago assured the youth.

"You may be right, *Abuelito*," Tip said, invariably calling the old man Little Grandfather although they were not related, "but not much of a one. Dad has been sworn into the posse Rastrow is taking with him. The marshal thinks that Silas Pine is still out there waiting for Ben Massingale to slip back to see his family."

"Rastrow," Santiago said harshly and paused to spit a stream of tobacco juice over his left arm. "Hee no ees my idea of a marshal."

"Nor Dad's either, to hear him tell it," Tip said, looping the lines over the wooden brake handle on the driver's side. "Nobody much likes him or his crew, 'cept maybe Horace Rogan."

"*Si,* Rastrow and thees odders, they are *Señor* Rogan's men, I theenk. Noah Pine wass a deecent man, *muchacho,* and eef *Señor* Pine, hee keel this man Banes, *por Dios,* you can bee essure hee had ver' good reeson."

All talk between the two stopped as Acting Marshal Rastrow himself eased in off the front street into the livery stable, clomping down the middle aisle.

"Listen up, Cruz," he said, pausing before the old Mexican. "I want three of the best saddle horses you've got here. Plenty of bottom, because we'll be pushin' 'em hard. An' I want 'em saddled *pronto.* Bring the best one over to the marshal's office right away. Keep the other two ready and waitin'. Reno Poteet and Black Ellis will be along for them soon's they can. Lefty Price is on his way now to get that wagon."

The marshal glared at Cruz, nodded his head at Tip Maginnis, and clomped back up the main aisle.

Santiago waited until the man's looming presence vanished out the stable door into the gray light of the cloudy day. Then he looked at Tip.

"You doo as thees marshal say, *muchacho*. Your *Abuelito* has a leetle erran' he moost run. I also have need for thee fast horse, but you moost tell no one where I am gone. Esay, eef they ask, I am gone to see thee joodge on beesness. No more, eh?"

"No more, *Abuelito*," Tip promised.

Autumn was a sad time of the year for Santiago Cruz who knew only too well the bitter cold and mountains of snow the winter would bring to this land. Late spring in the Wyoming high country saw the grass spread like a rich green carpet; bluebells and larkspurs, and delphinium spattered it with pink and blue and lavender. The sky would arch like a cobalt bowl, and an occasional chicken hawk or bald eagle could be seen swimming the high currents of the wind. Now all that was gone. The grass was turning brown. The flowers were gone. The leaves had begun to turn and to flutter swiftly away, whipped about by the wind. Thin groves of pine and juniper grew

110

tough and twisted from the shallow soil, interspersed by humpy belts of meadow.

The gray sky gave the land and all that was on it a pallor. The long flat on which the town was built began to peter out as the road mounted eastward into a range of low hills. They were formed by the remnants of ancient crags and flinty spires sculptured to weird shapes by the corrosion of time and weather. The road ahead became a series of switchbacks as the land climbed. Some of the rockier places were overgrown with tangles of brush and it was toward one of these that Santiago reined his zebra dun.

The posse would be riding ponderously and proudly along the stage road to the Massingale place. The route Santiago was taking was neither as fast nor as direct, but it would allow him to conceal his passage. If the *Señor Dios* smiled on him, his being in advance of the posse would give him a sufficient edge to get to the Massingale place in time to warn Shawn and Kerry Lu.

Ben Massingale was a bank robber and, now they said, a murderer as well. He had shot and killed Noah Pine in a running fight with the posse during a cloudburst and was a fugitive with a price on his head put there by the Grafton banker whose son, it was said, Ben or Sam Crowley had shot through the

111

back when making their escape from the bank. Santiago Cruz found that hard to believe. He had known and liked the young Easterner ever since he had settled on that small homestead ranch. Ben or Sam Crowley had never come to town without a kind word and nod for the hostler. Last Christmas Ben, who was always scrambling to make a go of it, had splurged and bought a Navajo rug from Mariana "to make our little home a little more cheerful." Mariana knew that the rug she had sold Ben had done just that since Shawn Massingale, next time she came to town, had made it a point to stop at their little house and compliment her on the workmanship.

The blanket *was* beautiful, a mixture of white handspun warp with indigo-dyed blue handspun and raveled red bayeta designs. Shawn had asked her the meaning of the various designs and Mariana had explained that they symbolized October, *Gah'ji*, the month of the back to back, the parting of the seasons. It is in this time that the deer come and it is time to hunt. *Nalashi*, the Tarantula, is its feather and *Nichi achi*, the Little Cold, is its heart. The blue bands stand for the blue haze hanging over this month. It is the time when women shell corn, thrash wheat, and store food for the winter.

This month and its symbols had once found

Shawn so happy, and now, thought Santiago mournfully, as it was approaching again, she could not be happy. No storing away of food for the winter. *Nichi achi* had Shawn and Kerry Lu held fast in his grasp. Even as he rode quickly around a rock outcropping and reined the zebra dun into a stand of trees that flanked the Massingale place he shrugged in irritation at himself. How possessed he had himself become with Mariana's Navajo beliefs, so much so that he had to admit, with regret, he had abandoned his Holy Mother in whose light he had been raised.

As he worked his way toward the edge of the stand of the trees, he saw Shawn and Kerry Lu mounting the rise of the stage road just beyond their place. In the distance he was able to distinguish the sounds of the mounted men in the posse, but the sounds suddenly ceased. As they did so, Shawn and Kerry Lu drew rein.

"*Señora, señorita,* com' queek. It is Santiago, your frien'. Thees men on the road ahead, they com' to take you prisoner. Queek, *por favor.* I know a way we go thees men weel not see us."

Shawn nodded her head, pulling her reins around and signaling Kerry Lu to follow her into the stand of trees where Santiago sat his horse, waiting anxiously. The bunched men

113

and horses just ahead on the road around a granite spire that had hidden them from view were in motion again. They pounded past the spot where Shawn was leaning forward to clamp the roan's nostrils, with Kerry Lu and Santiago doing likewise to their mounts. Reno Poteet and Isom Rastrow were in the vanguard, while Black Ellis brought up the rest of the men from the rear.

"Thees way, *Señora*," Santiago whispered in a rasping voice once the posse had spread out below, surrounding the little cabin and its outbuildings. He grinned, showing white teeth beneath the white mustache as he looked at Shawn's corduroy britches and Kerry Lu's dress tucked into her riding boots. "Even eef thees men see you at thees distance, *Señora*, I theenk they won' rec'gnize you."

He angled his way back through the stand of trees, the zebra dun proceeding very cautiously, the two women following, Kerry Lu in the middle, then her mother. None of them paused even for an instant to look back.

Chapter Twelve

Coming awake, Pine was alert in an instant. It was almost dawn. He had been dreaming, but not the recurring nightmare. He had been reliving the time the posse overtook Massingale and Crowley. The shot that killed Noah seemed so real it must have startled him out of his deep sleep.

Sitting up, he realized he actually felt more rested than at almost any time he could remember in the recent past. He'd slept like a baby and his body was loose and relaxed. Now he shook away his blankets and stood, glancing with satisfaction at Ben Massingale who was trussed up hand and foot, with the added precaution of both his wrists and ankles being tied to saplings that grew about six feet apart.

Massingale was uncomfortable in sleep, breathing through his open mouth. Occasionally a restless quiver rippled through his muscles. He, for certain, hadn't spent a restful night.

And he could remain that way a while longer. There was an edge on Silas Pine's appetite this morning, and he wanted to satisfy it ahead of anything else. He cooked up some bacon and pan bread and coffee, and then ate.

While he was finishing up half of what he'd prepared, Massingale stirred and groaned and slowly turned his head toward his captor.

"Would you mind?" he asked huskily. "Unless you intend to do me in after all, you'd better give me something to eat and drink."

Pine got up and, rifle in one hand and knife in the other, went over to Massingale and cut him free, keeping as much of the rope intact as he could for later use.

"All right, get up."

Massingale climbed to his feet, rubbing his wrists.

"I could stand to tramp around a little, sir. Loosen up a bit."

"Go ahead," Pine said. "Just do it slow and don't get too close to me, and don't try making a break. I'll shoot you if I have to."

"Yes."

Massingale seemed to exude an air of defeated compliance, but it was blunted by an attitude of cool disdain as he began tramping up and down the clearing.

He was a slightly built man of medium height, his face darkly weathered, his body muscular in a muted way. His manner was

116

polite, distant, withdrawn. His physical condition appeared worn and weary, his shirt and trousers stained with gritty dirt and sweat. Obviously he'd been living on tension alone all these days, wary of being captured. He had a full ragged mustache and beard; his thick hair was light brown and slightly curly.

Pine never took the leveled rifle off him. He had too much respect for the man's wilderness skills to underestimate him again.

"I'd like to eat now."

Pine nodded in the direction of the fire, and Massingale sat down beside it. Pine stood off at a short distance and watched him eat, and finally said out of pure curiosity: "You're a smart 'un, Mister. And a man'd judge you had a tall jag of learning, by the sound o' you."

"Well, I have." Massingale sopped some bacon grease with pan bread and took a swig of coffee. "Quite."

Whatever his personal feelings, the fugitive didn't appear inclined toward a surly silence. His demeanor seemed neutral and detached at the moment, but Pine wasn't fooled by it. *He'll be watching for any chance. And I'll be watching him.*

"Had a good education, you see. Came of an old and fairly well-to-do family in Great Britain. They saw to it that I received an excellent schooling at Cambridge University.

117

Then I shipped abroad without seeking their permission. Came to Boston."

"I wouldn't reckon," Pine said, "that was how you learned to get along so well in wild country."

"Not a bit of it. Once in America, I took every opportunity to get out of the city, roam the woods, savor life to the full. I suppose . . . ," Massingale paused thoughtfully as he poured another cup of coffee. "I suppose my family believed I was mostly trying to evade my responsibilities among the English gentry at home. It was never that. I wrote home frequently at first, but they never wrote back. I simply felt differently than they did. I wanted the freedom that getting away from civilization could offer me. And I found it."

That struck a responsive chord with Pine at once, but he suppressed any sign of it. "All the same, you married Miz Massingale. You begot yourself a daughter. You come West."

"Yes," Massingale agreed slowly. "Sometimes . . . well, it's a long story, but sometimes a thing may happen to a chap that will . . . change him. For me that something was Shawn. She's northern Irish, you know, Protestant and very British in her inclinations, so there was no question of a religious or political breach between us. I cared for her very much . . . and then I came up with the grand notion that the pair of us and Kerry Lu could make a new life out here."

He shook his head, bitterly and wryly.

"What a bloody fool I was! There's still wilderness in Massachusetts, but it's relatively tamed. None of it could have prepared us for what we came to encounter in your West. I trust you already know most of the rest. . . ."

Pine nodded. He and Massingale had spoken a little after he'd captured Ben last night. Massingale now fully understood why Pine had pursued him so relentlessly. What he didn't know was how Pine's own sense of guilt (for Ben's love of the wilderness and personal freedom ran so parallel with his own emotions) had been sharply renewed by their brief association.

Massingale had sacrificed almost all of his personal preferences for the sake of his wife and child. What had Silas Pine done except run away from his own?

Not lifting his head, Massingale said quietly, "I'm sorry about your son. He died in the thick of battle. It doesn't matter whether you believe me or not, I suppose. Your mind is made up. But the God's truth is that I usually hit what I aim at and I wasn't firing anywhere near him."

"Noah's dead. He was shot from in front.

119

Who am I supposed to believe killed him, if you didn't?"

Massingale was silent.

"Just like you say you got no loot out of Rogan's bank," Pine went on, staring at the other man fixedly. "Now that I've seen you, I know you hefted that sack on your horse as you rode out of town."

"Right you are," Massingale said, returning Pine's stare. "And I've told you that the sack had no money in it. Obbie Rogan said he'd have the money in a sack and hand it over to us as soon as we stuck him up. Maybe at one time that sack'd contained money, but not the sack I got buried at my camp. It was just cut-up paper and iron washers."

Pine grunted and motioned toward the dirty pans and dishes by the fire.

"Carry 'em to that spring yonder and scrub 'em. Then pack up everything. I'm taking you back to Grafton . . . but only after a little side trip to this camp of yours where you can dig up them washers and bring 'em along."

"You surely mean it."

"You damned right I do." Pine's voice was set and unrelenting. He was not about to be talked out of what he had seen with his own eyes and what had kept him on Massingale's trail these past days. "There's a court and law

120

to settle what will happen to you, if you don't make me kill you first. That's one thing I can do for sure. I aim to do it."

Chapter Thirteen

Isom Rastrow jerked abruptly awake. For a moment he wasn't sure what had brought him out of a dead sleep and then, culling his memory, he realized that it had been a gun shot. The echoes from it were still trailing along the ends of his nerves as he rolled out of his blankets, softly cursing.

Who the hell had fired that shot, and why?

Rastrow looked around him in the neutral light of pre-dawn. The sun was just edging up beyond the eastern hills. He saw that Reno Poteet's blankets were already thrown aside, and Poteet was gone. Because of how he'd suddenly awakened, Rastrow's brain was still working fuzzily, but seeing Poteet gone gave him a violent jolt to fresh awareness.

Black Ellis had led the posse in the direction that murdering Silas Pine had headed after leaving the Massingale place. Poteet and Ellis had caught up to them on the stage road just shortly before they had come to the rise before the Massingale place. No one seemed to think Poteet's story of having ridden over to check out the Crowley place first anything but the truth. Why should they? He and Ellis had actually come from the Crowley place, or at least near it, after they had sent Lefty Price and the Crowley woman in the wagon on to her shack and cut cross country to meet up with the posse.

Poteet and Rastrow were now in pursuit of Ben Massingale and had cut an even more direct approach up into the high country of the Neversummers rather than sticking to the old man's trail the way the posse was doing. That old fool had been moving slowly enough and they'd probably overtake him eventually. In the meantime, the two of them would have Massingale. Rastrow's first impulse on being awakened by the gun shot was one of nervous unease.

Was Massingale really that close by? He was a shrewd one in the wilds. And maybe Poteet had run into him by pure accident and been gunned down, the way that old piker had done for Bruno Banes. On his feet, Rastrow bent and picked up his rifle, and stood, waiting.

Presently Reno Poteet came barging roughly through a thicket, his rifle in one hand, grinning.

"What the hell was that shooting about?" Rastrow demanded.

"We need meat, don't we?"

"If we're going to stay on this hunt much

longer, sure. But I don't figure it'll be all that long. Something tells me Massingale is right near here."

"Mebbe. But I was havin' a hard time sleepin', so I got up, soon's it turned first light, and went out to see if I could bag us some small game."

"Yeah. I heard the shot. You fetch anything?"

"Not 'xactly." Poteet rubbed a hand over his whiskered jaw, still grinning. "Seen a bear, Isom, one huge son of a bitch. Standin', I'd wager he was ten, mebbe twelve feet tall. Could pervide us with meat fer a long spell. So, I shot 'im. Got him right below his right front shoulder. But the shot didn't kill 'im. He jest charged away into some underbrush. Didn't get no chance fer another shot at 'im."

"That's fine," Rastrow said in heavy disgust. "Now we got ourselves a wounded bear out there and it might turn on anybody. Including us."

Poteet looked mildly hurt.

"Hell, Isom, you ever heerd of a bear turnin' on a human bein'? A he-bear?"

"No," Rastrow said, "not that I know of. Unless this wasn't no he-bear. Maybe it was a *she*-bear and she had cubs close by. If that was the case, she'd be likely to tear up anybody got near to her after this."

Poteet took off his hat, blinked and scratched his head kind of sheepishly, then resumed his grin.

"You know somep'n? That never crossed my mind."

Rastrow reached for patience. "No, I don't figure it did, Reno. But it gives us something else to worry about, don't it?"

"Mebbe," Poteet said. "But not jest us, Isom. You fergetting that Massingale is out there somewheres? Might be, if it was a she-bear, she'll save us a whole lot of huntin'."

Rastrow shrugged with indifference.

"Best we get to making our vittels and then hit the trail."

It wasn't until mid morning that Shawn Massingale emerged from the tall-growing brush near a crag that overlooked the night camp in which the new marshal and his deputy had spent the previous night. She was afoot, having left her roan horse sheltered back in the trees. She made her way cautiously to where there had been a fire and, while no woodsman like Ben, she could tell from the ashes that she wasn't more than two hours behind them.

She had an advantage they didn't, the posse didn't, Silas Pine didn't. Ben had told her where his camp was located and how to get to it if an emergency arose. Without probably knowing it, those two had been within ten miles of the secluded cave beneath a knobby peak the other side of the Navajo encampment where Massingale was forted up. Very early that morning she had heard a shot, just one, and had wondered if it had meant discovery. But now she was sure it hadn't. These men were too far away, unless Ben had crept down for a look at them and had been seen and they had taken a shot at him. But it wasn't like Ben to be seen when he didn't want anyone to see him. The fact that he'd been at liberty for this long without anyone finding him more than proved that.

Half way back to town, Shawn had paused to take her leave of Kerry Lu and Santiago. It would not do for anyone from town to see her. Let them think that she had abandoned Kerry Lu and Santiago had found her riding toward Grafton and brought her back with him alone.

Shawn had expected Kerry Lu to start crying and had been surprised when she didn't, although she knew her daughter well enough to realize the tears weren't very far beneath the surface. It was only that Dad needed help and there was no one but Mom any more to help him. He wouldn't leave without Shawn and she wouldn't leave without him. Together, they might make it. If they did, Kerry Lu could join them and they could all start life over in a new place. It wasn't much, but it was the only hope any of them had any more, and so they believed it with a fervor that kept them from admitting, aloud anyway, any fears or doubts.

With a *"vaya con Dios"* from Santiago, Shawn had headed up the sharp rise which ran alongside the trail. It wasn't until she was safely hidden by the trees and could rein in the roan without being seen that Shawn had looked back and saw the pair of them retreating into the distance, old Santiago's back hunched forward, Kerry Lu riding straight in the saddle, swaying slightly as her mule moved, less than a horse-length behind the Mexican. Her eyes blurred with tears, then, as for the first time she let the terror of what she was doing assail her, and thought, truly, this might be the last time she would ever see her daughter.

Back now beside her roan, checking the loads in the revolver, her eyes blurred again as she remembered Kerry Lu's riding off into the distance. If those men ahead, or if Pine, came between her and her man, so help her God, she'd kill them, or she'd die trying. Ben, Kerry Lu, their life together was all she had to live for, and she wasn't willing to give it up, *not as long as she could fight*. That fierce determination burned the tears from her eyes, even as she rubbed the residue from her cheeks, reddened from emotion as much as from the sharp wind which was blowing. Climbing into the saddle, she urged the roan forward, moving confidently now across the small deserted clearing.

Chapter Fourteen

It had turned very cold during the night and a wind was blowing briskly. It seemed that all at once the leaves had turned. The maples were a brilliant gold, the cottonwoods and alders a mixture of red and yellow with still a suggestion of green. There was also a dampness in the air, coming down off the Neversummers.

Horace Rogan kept pulling his short-brimmed Stetson down more firmly on his head as he walked swiftly, then hugging his broadcloth coat closely about him to keep out the chill. His eyes traveled nervously, almost desperately ahead of him, with single-minded purpose.

He had been shaken to the very depths by what Helen Gates had told him that morning in the kitchen. He had been so intent on wanting Ben Massingale dead that he was now in even a greater quandary than he had been in the hours just before the robbery. It was not just that Massingale was said to have been the man who had shot Obbie during the holdup. For any father to be filled with feelings of hatred and a desire for revenge over the loss of a son, even if in his case a son toward whom he had felt only a well-concealed contempt, was natural enough to justify to everyone in Grafton the reward he had posted for the small rancher's capture. Only, with Isom Rastrow and his men charged with that capture, he was certain Massingale would be brought in dead.

For one thing, Massingale was not likely to give himself up. Rogan suspected he was the only one among the posse members who knew for a fact that it had not been Ben's shot that had downed Noah Pine. As far as Horace Rogan was concerned, this knowledge was his hole card. Massingale was sure to be killed, if not by Rastrow, then by that crazy mountain man father of Noah's.

Ben Massingale must die. He had said it over and over to himself, and to others. The reason for his saying it was so evident to everyone that Rogan had been secretly amused. With Massingale dead, there would be no chance of the sack supposedly containing over ten thousand dollars in money belonging to the bank's depositors ever surfacing again. Horace Rogan knew where that money was and he knew it was not in any sack carried off by Massingale or Crowley. He had made sure of that early the morning of the robbery.

But for all that, he had been convinced in his heart that it had probably been Massingale's bullet that had killed Obbie. Now to learn from Mrs. Gates that Aurelia Crowley insisted that Ben had not murdered Obbie opened the door to too many unpleasant possibilities. If not Massingale, if not Crowley, if not Jake Milton or Asa Blayde, then who?

The thought was doubly terrifying because his mind had at once jumped to the same person who had coldly plugged Noah Pine in all the confusion, the rain, and wind, and darkness, and the gunfire. He had said nothing at the time, nor later. He was keeping that information back and would only use it if it proved to be to his advantage.

As it was Hal Owen, Judge Tabor, and the other depositors were out a few thousands. They would survive. But as little as he had thought of him when alive, it dismayed Rogan to think that Obbie's death had been something other than accidental, something other than the ironic working of fate and a sardonic twist of retributive justice. If Obbie had been murdered by someone other than the frustrated and impoverished little ranchers with whom he had conspired, Horace Rogan was not so much a fool as not to realize that the knowledge which he had been regarding as his hole card might conceivably mean his finish as well. He had a new reason to congratulate himself for having kept quiet about what he knew.

He crossed the dirt street and opened the gate in the white picket fence that ran across the front yard and down the sides of the little house where Helen Gates and her daughter lived. It was a modest, unpretentious dwelling, and the Grafton Bank held the mortgage on it. Somehow, it was impossible for Horace Rogan to look upon anything or anybody without calculating the bank's role, either potentially or in fact. It was the promise of money, with a substantial downpayment from Isom Rastrow, which had prompted him to begin the machinery of eviction which had played so conveniently into Obbie's plan and had given him willing ears rather than skepticism when he had made his overture to those small ranchers faced with financial and personal ruin.

There was a ruffled curtain around the inside of the half glass in the front door and a knocker mounted on the door frame. Rogan banged it loudly in his agitated state. He wasn't even sure what he was going to say to Aurelia, but he had somehow to find out how much she knew and how accurate was her knowledge. When there was no response, he knocked again, and again.

From somewhere inside the little house he heard a baby beginning to cry. Yes, that's right. The Crowleys did have a baby. Now how was he to have a private conversation with the mother with the baby crying? He knocked this time with his knuckles against the door. There was still no answer, but the wailing of the baby seemed to intensify.

Giving up on the front door, Rogan began to circle the house, thinking that perhaps Aurelia was out back and couldn't hear either his knocking or her baby crying. The flowers by the side of the house were all withered, dry stalks being buffeted now by the unrelenting wind.

The small back yard was deserted. No one stood by the well. Thinking that perhaps Aurelia was in the outhouse, he walked over to the small, gray clapboard structure and called out.

"Miz Crowley? Are you in there?"

Silence.

It was then he saw that the small wooden latch was turned so that the door could not be opened. Obviously, Aurelia must be somewhere in the house.

Tramping along the short path to the back porch, Rogan became aware again of the wailing child inside.

"That kid sure has one powerful set of

lungs," he remarked to himself as he paused to tap now on the rear door. When there was no answer, he touched the porcelain knob, turned it, and to his surprise the door opened.

The kitchen was deserted. Horace Rogan could see the tea cups and saucers and other dishes neatly stacked near the sink. Someone had done the morning dishes.

A quick look in the parlor showed that room also to be empty. As he made his way down the narrow hallway to the bedrooms, Rogan again called out Aurelia's name. There was only the baby's wailing.

Entering the smaller bedroom, the banker walked over to the baby crib off to one side. It was old and had probably been Susan's when she was a baby. As he leaned over and looked at Baby Hope, he was surprised that she suddenly had stopped crying. She stared up at him in silence. There were tears in her eyes, but no fear.

Afterwards, he never knew why it had happened. After all, this was somebody else's baby, and a black baby at that, but he reached out to her and gently lifted her into his arms.

Horace Rogan hadn't held a baby since Obbie had been an infant, and then Sarah had always objected. "Put down that baby," she had said. "What if you were to drop him?" But she hadn't held him much herself. She didn't believe in encouraging Obbie if he was crying. The only cure for that, she had said, was to let him cry it out and see it wasn't going to get him anything.

Now, holding Baby Hope very close to him, Horace Rogan smiled at her and with one big finger touched her chin and then stroked her torso. It pleased him as few things had ever pleased him in his life when Baby Hope smiled back at him.

He began to mumble nonsense to her, and pace about the floor, being careful to keep Baby Hope near his body so she would be warm. Sticking out her tongue at him, as she was wont to do, saliva bubbled from her tiny mouth. With great care, Rogan used the bodice of Baby Hope's night shirt to dry her lips.

"What a darling little cap you have on," he cooed then, and pulled a flap on one side more tightly down on her little head. Instinctively, keeping one hand beneath her head and supporting Baby Hope's fragile body with the other, he made his way into the parlor. Flipping his head about so his own small-brimmed Stetson tumbled to the floor, he laughed at this antic, and began to make high humming sounds, as high as he could raise his rather gravelly voice. Baby Hope seemed to find the sound soothing.

He was sitting in the padded rocking chair

in the corner of the parlor next to the Franklin stove, smiling but no longer humming, when he saw Susan Gates coming up the front walk hours later. Baby Hope had fallen asleep in his arms and he would not stir even to open the front door because he felt any movement might awaken her.

Chapter Fifteen

"It's buried about a thousand yards above here," Massingale said.

His hands were tied in front so he could hold the reins of the horse he rode. A rope was also looped beneath the horse's barrel, tying his feet together. A third, longer rope, was around Massingale's neck and tied at the other end to Pine's pack horse which had remained between the two men as they had ascended to the elevation where Massingale had made his camp. These tethers made their passage slow, but also secure. The fugitive would not be bolting toward freedom.

Pine held his reins in his left hand and supported the rifle resting in the crook of his left arm. His right was free to swing the rifle to his shoulder and fire should Massingale attempt to make a break for freedom. It was also likely that the plodding pack horse would balk, snapping the man's neck in the process.

All three horses now were standing in a small clearing near which Pine could see and hear the swift rushing of a mountain creek. There was a cluster of plum trees at the far edge of the clearing and the plums swinging from the branches were small but blood ripe. The wind had died to an occasional flutter and there was the oppression of cold rain in the thin mountain air.

"We can't get there on horses," Massingale said, looking earnestly back over his left shoulder at Pine.

"Then we go on foot," Pine said, shifting his rifle to his right hand as he slowly dismounted, never allowing his eyes to waver from the other man.

He walked forward toward the pack horse. He again crooked the rifle in his left arm as he pulled at the rope tied to Massingale's neck.

"This rope stays on, by grab," he muttered, "so just ease yourself out of that saddle."

Massingale did as he was told until he was standing beside the brown horse he had been riding. He looked around briefly and then back at Pine who had edged a horse's length away.

"I wasn't going to tell you this," he said in an off-handed manner that somehow also conveyed a degree of embarrassment, "but there's a she-bear with cubs 'round here. Now, normally, she avoids humans as much as we avoid she-bears. I figured her being around would protect my camp and my cache — as if it needed protecting."

Pine grunted his disbelief and signaled with his head for Massingale to take the lead.

Their passage was almost noiseless on the needle-carpeted ground. Presently, through the tree trunks, a gray pinnacle came into sight. Pine could see that it was part of a wedge-shaped mass of granite that jutted steeply upward.

Massingale skirted widely to the right of this formation, working around northeast of the pinnacle. They trekked through a lonely clump of aspens and emerged at a small clearing with the mouth of a cave off slightly to the left.

"That's where the she-bear's been hanging out," Massingale said in a soft voice.

Pine was fatigued from the elevation and the climb and his breath came harshly. There was almost no movement of the air here and Pine detected an odd smell in the vicinity, a combination of mashed chokecherries and musky dog. He knew what that meant and he edged closer to Massingale.

"I don't want you going near that cave," he told Massingale.

"Don't intend to," Ben said, still speaking in a soft voice. "The cache is buried under that aspen about thirty feet from the cave."

"You going to need something to dig with?"

"No, I dug out a hole under a root, buried

139

the washers, and put a rock over the top. It should be easy to dig it up again."

Pine had his rifle in his right hand now, so positioned that it would be an easy matter to swing it up and shoot from the hip. His left hand held the end of the rope.

"Just take it very easy," he said. "I'll be right behind you."

Massingale proceeded to the aspen tree he had indicated. Falling to his knees, he bent forward and dug his fingers into the earth at the sides of a piece of granite. He had done a good job of concealment, Pine had to admit, since it did not seem to have been disturbed. Pulling up the rock with a backward thrust, Massingale rolled it over to one side. Then he reached into the hole and pulled out a gray canvas bag with the words Grafton Bank printed on it in black letters. Undoing the cord which bound the bag, Massingale spilled out part of its contents. He'd been right. Washers. Several sizes of them. Some as large as a double-eagle, some as small as a five-dollar gold piece. Some were as small and thin as gold dollars.

Pine had been on the alert every moment since he had first detected the odd smell, but the sight of the washers distracted him.

"There's the lot of the bank's money . . . ," Massingale began, but stopped.

Behind them, at just about the spot where they had first stood surveying the small clearing, was a tremendous silver-tipped gray she-grizzly. Hearing what had sounded like a great belch, Pine had twisted his head away from Massingale. Now he saw the grizzly with a tumbler's jerk of her mighty body rise up before them on two legs. From the mouth of the cave poured out two little brown grizzly cubs who ran toward their mother, ducking behind her now, cowering and whimpering.

Blood had been gushing down from her left rear hip and it had clotted in her fur. The massive beast began straddling toward the two men, her huge head humped down into her thick neck.

She had a piggish snout and a dog-like mouth, opening and drooling. If she was in pain, it didn't seem to slow her progress any. Her musky smell permeated the air.

Pine dropped backward in terror, leaving go of the rope and swinging his rifle up to fire a shot. His breath caught.

Standing on two legs, the grizzly was as huge as a bull. It was because of her hugeness that her progress toward them had appeared to be so slow. She was actually moving at incredible speed.

Time froze for Silas Pine. He was sighting her with the rifle when she roared. It seemed that she was looming too close for him to get a fair shot at her, the fur on her silver neck ruffled and humped, her silver head now gazing with mean eyes down at him, several feet above him and way too near.

Pine had raised his rifle quickly, but the bear was faster yet. Her ivory-gray claws, each as long as a man's finger, but curved a little like iron hooks, had been closing and unclosing, the pink dugs visible. Now, swinging in a roundhouse, just as Pine was about to pull the trigger, one of her mighty paws struck the rifle, flinging it out and away from Pine. It flashed through Pine's terrified consciousness that she must have recognized the weapon, recognized it and believed it was the same weapon which had wounded her.

What if my heart gives out now? Pine thought.

But even as this thought came to him, his left hand flicked to the scabbard holding his Green River. Still backing away from the grizzly, he sent the knife flying, not at the mighty beast, but sideways, toward Massingale. It stuck in the ground in front of Ben.

"Cut them ropes, boy!" Pine shouted. "Save yourself."

Retreating as swiftly as he could, Silas now drew out his Colt revolver.

Again the grizzly was too fast for him. She seemed to know what that was for also. With

142

her other paw, she batted it away. Silas jumped back to avoid that flashing paw and his heels hit a jutting rock. He fell over backwards, fell hard. His peaked black Stetson flew backwards behind him.

With more speed than he had mustered in a long time, Pine rolled sideways, and managed to leap to his feet again. The huge bear was almost on top of him. With her right paw she slammed him on the side of the head, her talons raking across his ear and along his jaw, ripping into his scalp. This blow sent Pine half-somersaulting into the air before he again hit the ground, hard.

"Keep away from her, Pine!" Massingale screamed, cutting and tearing at the rope around his wrists. It had been worked loose some in the ride up here and even more so in digging around the rock and rolling it aside.

Miraculously, Pine was once more on his feet. All those years in the rough, all the experienced muscles he had, and all his energy were now paying off. Backpedaling before the grizzly, she seemed ten feet tall to him and then her silver shape began to blur before his eyes, magnifying her, making her seem twice as tall, three times.

The she-grizzly, still on two legs, both paws held at the ready to cuff, came at him. She roared.

In his desperation Pine realized that he had no weapons with which to battle her. His last chance, the knife, he had flipped toward Massingale. That bit of altruism was about to cost him his life. *What there was left of it.*

That's right, he thought. It *is* almost over for me anyway.

The she-grizzly could move faster than he could going backwards, or even probably in an all-out forward run. When the great right paw took another swipe at him, Pine leaped suddenly, not backward, but forward, getting inside her reach. From his left pocket he had dug out his clasp knife. Burrowing his face into her chest fur, nearly overcome by the musky smell, he managed to get it open. The clubbing paw swung around, missing him instead of batting him. His face was pressed so tightly against the bear's body that one of her dugs squirted milk over him. It ran down the side of his face, the side without the blood seeping from his scalp, ear, and jaw, and trickled down into his clothing.

But he had the clasp knife open now, with its three-inch blade.

She roared above him, around him; he could hear the roar inside her mighty chest. She roared and kept roaring, clawing clumsily at him. Her ivory-gray claws brought up strips of his clothing and strips of living flesh from his back. Yet Pine wrapped his arms about her as tightly as he could, the open clasp-knife now in his right hand, buried to the hilt in her deep fur and probably no more than pricking her flesh.

She clawed at him clumsily and kept roaring. Suddenly, Pine's right hand flew backwards and then upwards, holding onto the knife and reaching as high above his head as he could. This time the knife plunged up to the hilt into the soft blackness of her snout.

The she-grizzly roared in agony and enraged pain. Blood was now spurting over Pine's hand. The bear jerked her head away, the knife remaining stuck in the soft flesh of her nose. The paws went up and clapped together about the hilt of the knife. Pine chose this moment to pull back. The knife still in her nose, her body heaving with the roar of her pain, the bear bent forward and seized his head in her open jaws. Pine felt himself being lifted from his feet.

The sound of the gunfire went unnoticed. Each bullet Massingale, who had managed to free himself, fired plunged into the back of the hulking giant. She only swung her huge head back and forth, Pine's head still gripped in her mouth. Pine could feel the sharp dog-teeth crunch into his skull. The way a cat might shake a mouse, the she-grizzly now shook Silas Pine. His body dangled crazily. His neck cracked. He screamed as Massingale continued to fire shot after shot from the repeating rifle into her, the last shot hitting her just below the heart. Pine lapsed into unconsciousness and the she-grizzly dropped him in a heap.

She now turned directly on Massingale and charged at him, blood spouting from her back, from her chest, from her nose where the knife, finally having worked loose, dangled and with a final shake of her head flew off into the nearby brush. Ben knew he had only time for one more shot, so swiftly was the gigantic bear moving toward him. He aimed this time for the head, squeezed the trigger.

It seemed that as the bullet smashed into her brain the bear was upon him. She staggered drunkenly and then, from her great height, came crashing to the earth, falling directly on him where he stood. He began losing consciousness as a rumble came deeply from within her body and two or three shots were fired, the baby cubs whimpering and screaming. Then silence. Then nothing.

Chapter Sixteen

Lefty Price was uncomfortable. Something deep inside of him rebelled at pistol-whipping a woman, even a black woman. There was a bluish contusion that had formed around the caked and dried blood on Aurelia Crowley's left temple where she'd been struck.

It bothered Lefty that in the long ride out from town to the Crowley hovel, the woman had not regained consciousness. He didn't personally have much use for doctors of any kind, including Injun medicine men, but he knew enough about blows to the head that they could be fatal or, worse, that a person might never come to if hit hard in a certain way.

He was fearful that was what had happened to Aurelia Crowley.

There was a patina of sweat on his brow and the tuft of hair beneath his Stetson stuck clammily to his bald scalp. The hovel was not even all that warm despite the fire he had built in the old black stove in order to boil water in a battered kettle with a metal handle. By the time the water had come to a boil that handle was too hot to touch. He had burned his left hand slightly just brushing across it and then had to look for a rag of some kind to wrap around the handle so he could pour some of the water into a basin he had found on a shelf.

Lefty wasn't certain in his own mind why he should use hot water to cleanse a wound, instead of cold, except that he had seen it done that way once and figured that there was probably a good reason for it.

The Crowleys were so poor that they evidently couldn't afford a bedstead and instead had slept on a double mattress stretched across the dirt floor in a far corner of the shack. It was onto this mattress that Price had gently lowered Aurelia Crowley's inert body after carrying her in from the wagon.

Her breathing, at least, was shallow and rapid, so she wasn't dead. But, beyond that. . . .

Price kneeled down beside the mattress. He had cut some shavings off a bar of lye soap and mixed it up with the hot water in the basin. Taking off his neckerchief from around his neck, he soaked one end of it in the soapy water and then, with surprising delicacy for one with such short, stubby fingers and hands scarred and rope-burned from years of working with tough mustangs, he removed the crusted blood. With great care, he daubed the wound and then rinsed the bandanna in the soapy water before applying it again to the bruised area. An element of desperation had entered Price as he looked at the reclining body with ever mounting nervous tensity. There was a bluish discoloration to the woman's lips and beneath the nails of her fingers. Although her face seemed pinched, there was no real expression. Her breathing was still rapid but very shallow.

He wanted to speak to her. He wanted her to come out of it. He wasn't sure why he cared so much about whether or not she lived, but he did.

Even had he not been so intently preoccupied he probably would not have heard Opal Cameron's black mare on the packed ground of the compound outside. She was living now with the Navajos and Gage had taught her how to approach any place that held potential danger with a stealth that had become second nature to her. Opal's baby had been burned to death in the cabin she had occupied with her first husband, Reeve Bedoe, in a neighboring valley. The Crowleys being former slaves, as she and Reeve had been, presented the occasion for her to make an initial friendly overture, but what had cemented her relationship with Aurelia had been Aurelia's infant.

"Where's Baby Hope?" she asked, standing

in the doorway. The wind outside pulled so strongly that she had had to lean forward when walking in it. In one hand, she held the latch of the front door; in the other hand she held a Colt Double-Action Frontier revolver with a long barrel.

"Who . . . ?" was as far as Lefty Price got, whipping his head around suddenly on hearing the strange voice. Then he just gaped. He had never seen anything like this before.

Opal Cameron was about twenty-seven and almost pure black. She was tall and lean and dressed in soft leather pants dyed black with small silver hemispheres set closely together up the outer seams. Over her upper body she wore a heavy serape with the characteristic Navajo black and white stripes and diamonds over her breasts. The shirt beneath was white cotton. Around her forehead she wore a red and yellow *banda* holding down her long hair, surprisingly straight compared to Aurelia's kinky curls. More handsome than beautiful, her face had long lines with high cheekbones and her eyes were almond-colored and flashed as she regarded Lefty Price, the Colt held confidently and thrust slightly forward. Now she cocked the hammer all the way back with a thumb.

"I asked you a question, white man!"

"What . . . who is . . . baby what?"

"What have you done with this woman's baby?"

"I don't know nothin' about no baby. I ain't seen no baby. Honest."

Opal Cameron came far enough into the one-room hovel that she was able to push the door closed behind her, against the wind which tugged at it, and leaned her back against it.

"You've got little time left to you, white man, if you don't answer my question. I shot the white man who killed my baby and if you've hurt Baby Hope you'll get the same."

Lefty's kneeling position was becoming awkward for him, but he had enough self-possession not to move. This black woman who looked to him more like an Indian than a Negro had about her a quiet menace that was totally unsettling. The almond eyes watched him with calm, half-aloof pride.

"My job was to watch over this woman until the marshal gets back here. That's all I know. They got her from a house in town and I brought her out in that wagon over yonder."

"In that condition?"

"It was none of my doin', believe me. I wasn't even in the house with them others. She was like that when Reno and Black carried her out to the wagon. That's where I was

151

sittin' while they went inside to get her."

"Reno and Black?"

"Deputies, ma'am, like I am."

"You're a deputy?" Opal said in such a tone that the word curdled.

"Yes'm. Sworn in by Marshal Rastrow hisself. That's the lay of it. This here is a sort of stopping off place fer her until she comes around."

"And then what?"

"Then she is . . . ah, to be escorted off this range and sent packing, I guess."

"Without Baby Hope?"

"I told you, I don't know anything about no baby. I don't really know nothin' about this here Negress, 'cept that the marshal wants her kept outta harm's way for a spell."

Lefty Price's face reddened as he tried to explain what he didn't really understand himself all that well. The story sure sounded phony — even to him — and he was telling it.

"On your feet, mister, and turn your back to me. Not fast, mind you. This pistol of mine has a hair-trigger."

Lefty, using his hands braced against a knee, raised his squat body to a standing position and turned his back toward what he was sure now was the blackest Injun he'd ever hope to see.

Opal came forward with a sinuous grace Lefty could not see and couldn't even hear for so silently did she move. He knew she was near only when he felt his own revolver tugged swiftly from his holster.

"You stay the way you are," the intimidating voice said from somewhere behind him, "and put out your wrists behind you."

"You're not gonna hog-tie me, are you ma'am?"

"Rather be shot?"

"No."

"Then, let's see the wrists."

Lefty Price thrust out his arms behind his back, his wrists close together. He felt a thin reata of pliable rawhide encircle them and then, with a few deft twists, encircle them thrice more before being pulled taut.

"On your belly, now," the voice said. "Keep your eyes on that wall there while you're doing it."

Lefty obeyed and presently his ankles were quickly tied together and bound tightly to the rawhide around his wrists.

Aurelia Crowley moaned softly.

It was the first sound Lefty Price had heard her make. Despite his predicament, he felt a sudden rush of relief. Maybe she'd be coming out of it now.

He felt himself being dragged swiftly across

153

the dirt floor. This Indian woman had amazing strength for one so lean.

Price was rolled toward the wall near the door.

"Don't look around," the tall black woman warned. "I am called Hears with Hawk's Ears among the *Dineh*. Just keep studying that wall."

Price muttered his assent. The moaning was more frequent. He could hear that much, and the tall woman's murmuring.

Aurelia Crowley's eyes fluttered open. Her eyes seemed to be staring, but they had no luster and her pupils were so dilated her irises seemed to have vanished. She appeared, without really seeing her, to be aware of Opal's lean form squatting beside her.

"Opal? How did yo'-all happen to come by?"

Then she became more aware of her surroundings, with those staring eyes.

"How'd Ah get back to de place, Opal? I don' recall yo' bringin' me."

"I didn't," Opal said quietly. "He did."

She pointed toward the man trussed up and rolled with his face to the wall near the door.

"Who de devil is he? Ah've never done seen dat man befo'."

"Then he wasn't the one who hit you?"

Aurelia tried to move her right arm, but

154

couldn't. Her eyes were squinched and her face still held no expression.

"No, dat was one o' dem deputties, two o' 'em, but none dressed like dat man over dere."

She told Opal all she could remember of what had happened to her in the Gates's kitchen until the moment she had waked up on her own mattress in her own home. It didn't take long. Suddenly Aurelia rolled her head in the direction of the bound man.

"Hope?! What did dat man do wit' mah baby?"

"Maybe he'll be more willing to talk now," Opal said, rising and moving in Price's direction. "If not, his kind have taught me ways of dealing with that, too."

She smiled as she said it, a smile not visible to Aurelia on the mattress, but it was to Lefty who had been craning his head around so he could watch what was happening. Aurelia's breathing was still rapid and shallow and, suddenly, it seemed to fill the room. She moaned gently, so that Opal stopped in midcourse on her way toward Lefty and turned swiftly toward the mattress.

She moved back and squatted beside Aurelia and stretched out her hand to feel the other woman's chest. Aurelia Crowley had stopped breathing. Her eyes, still open, were blank, staring emptily toward the ceiling. Even the lobes of her ears were blue.

A shudder passed palpably through that small room. Even Lefty Price felt it. The eyes he turned toward the wall were filled with tears. But this was nothing to the terror he felt when he heard Opal rise again to her feet and begin walking toward him.

Chapter Seventeen

Isom Rastrow had every reason to be proud of himself as he rode before the posse on the road that led to town. Just behind him, Reno Poteet rode Silas Pine's big horse, balancing the scarcely conscious body of Ben Massingale in front of him. They had run into Black Ellis and the posse shortly after they had started down from the Neversummers camp with the fugitive Massingale in tow.

They had dumped old Silas Pine's gear to the ground and they had left the old bastard to die of his wounds and exposure. A bullet found in the body of the dead marshal's father might raise questions, even if the man had been wanted for the murder of Deputy Bruno Banes. This way, they'd just find his bones picked clean by the birds and the wolves and the coyotes, next to the carcass of the giant she-bear they had brought down when it was mauling Massingale. Reno had sent a couple of slugs through the cubs for good measure.

Originally, Poteet had wanted to bring one of the cubs back as a souvenir, if he couldn't chop off the head of the she-bear; but Rastrow had nixed both ideas. Getting Massingale down in one piece so he could tell them the location of the bank money would be enough of a job in itself. After that, Massingale could either die of his wounds, or get himself killed trying to escape.

Rastrow had never been closer to that money than he was right now. And he needed that money. Without it, he couldn't swing the deal with Rogan to buy the four homesteads and throw them together into a horse ranch. Now, he would have the bank money and the reward Rogan had posted for Massingale's capture.

It brought a wisp of a smile to Isom Rastrow's lips as he thought of how he would end up with the horse ranch he had wanted for years and all of it paid for by Horace Rogan and Rogan's bank.

The wind hadn't really let up since beginning their descent. It pushed the brims of their Stetsons back against the crowns, blew the manes of the horses, and made their eyes burn and smart. The sky was overcast but it had not rained. It might be snowing up in the Neversummers, though. Right now, Silas Pine might be moldering under a layer of snow, the blood that had been leaking out of him freezing on the ground.

"Hey, boss, whaddya think's goin' on?"

Black Ellis asked.

He had spurred his horse up until he was riding now alongside Rastrow as they entered the main street of Grafton. The marshal's office and jail was on this end of town, about a block from the Grafton Livery Stable and Feed Barn, but on the other side of the street. There was quite a crowd congregated around the marshal's office.

"Dunno," Rastrow told Ellis. "Mebbe word got out we caught Massingale."

"I don't think that's it, boss."

"Well, let's take a *pasear* over and see," Rastrow said, and he clucked to his mount to increase its pace.

Santiago Cruz was outside the door with two kids, Tip Maginnis and a girl about twelve that looked to be Ben Massingale's daughter, Kerry Lu. As Rastrow reined up before the hitchrack, he could see old Judge Llewellyn Tabor's white head just inside the doorway, his daughter Malinda standing next to him in her usual outfit of Quaker gray. The judge had on a dark brown frock coat.

"Say, Mex, what's goin' on here?" Rastrow called out, as he began to dismount.

"Thay have caught the *hombre* who estole and keeled poor *Señora* Crowley, *Señor* Marshal," Cruz said in too loud a voice. "Thees *hombre*, hee wass one of your deeputies, no?"

159

"One of my deputies?" Rastrow said angrily, shoving forward. "What the hell kind of greaser talk is that?"

"Is that Acting Marshal Rastrow?" Judge Tabor's voice called from inside the office.

"Yeah, it is," Rastrow said, pushing Cruz aside as he strode through the narrow doorway in to the marshal's office. Black Ellis was right behind him. "We're back from capturing Ben Massingale. Got him in tow outside. . . ."

He stopped speaking then. The small office was crammed with people. Horace Rogan was standing off to the side, rocking what appeared to be a black baby in his arms. Next to him stood Rawina Pine, her sharp, bitter features lighted by curious, nervous eyes. Susan and Helen Gates were there as well, standing next to the judge whose right hand was on Malinda's left arm, and over before the two-cell jail a tall black woman dressed like an Indian held the jail door keys in her grip. Her almond-colored eyes flashed at Isom Rastrow.

"Who the hell are you?" Rastrow rasped at her. "What is all this?"

Then, as Opal Cameron moved aside slightly, Rastrow saw Lefty Price sitting on the mattress of the iron cot chained to the wall inside the cell farthest to the left.

"I'm Opal Cameron," the tall black woman said. "The man in the cell is charged with the murder of Aurelia Crowley."

"The devil you say." Rastrow's face blanched. "How do you know she's dead? And who says my deputy did it?"

"I do," Opal said. "I found him and Aurelia Crowley out at the Crowley place. She's dead. I brought her body back to town in the same wagon this man used to take her out there. The body's over at Doc Whitelaws's office."

"If Miz Crowley's dead, I'd believe you killed her before I'd believe Lefty Price did." Rastrow's tone sounded hollow even to himself, but he arched his back stubbornly. "I haven't seen you around these parts."

"I've known Opal Cameron from the time she first came to this territory," Rawina Pine put in, walking over to confront Rastrow. Her hands were red as were her cheeks. Her black eyes were piercing. "I know her a sight better than I know you or your henchmen."

"The woman's all right, Isom," Horace Rogan said, still holding the baby cradled in his arms. "The bank will vouch for her. Her husband discovered a pocket of gold on the Los Pinos. His family's very well off now. Opal here and her husband, Gage, decided to keep only a little of the gold for themselves. They've gone to live with old Adakhai and his Navajos."

"Gage Cameron," Rastrow said, pushing

back his Stetson so it rested above his forehead. "Seems I remember hearin' 'bout him. He's a 'breed, ain't he?"

"And me?" Opal asked archly. "I'm that 'breed's wife."

"You may be," Rastrow admitted, "but dressed like an Injun or not, you're just another nigger to me. And I don't trust niggers. I never have."

Opal's hand leaped out so swiftly it beat the indignant words Rawina Pine was about to spit at the lawman. It connected with Isom Rastrow's left cheek and there was a resounding clap throughout the room.

Black Ellis went for his gun instinctively, and then suddenly paused.

"I wood not doo that, *Señor*," Santiago Cruz said. "My *pistola*, she ees in your baak and I weel pool thee trigger, beelieve mee."

Rastrow, rubbing his cheek with his left hand, turned abruptly toward where Black Ellis was standing, now with Santiago Cruz behind him, his gun drawn.

"Put it away, Mex, or you'll be sharing a cell with Massingale."

"You caught him, then?" Rogan asked, even in his excitement not relinquishing the baby.

"Did you happen to see my former husband, Marshal?" Rawina Pine asked.

162

Rastrow shifted his eyes angrily to Opal Cameron.

"If'n there's one thing that don't set well with me, it's an uppity nigger, even if she is wearin' Injun feathers!"

Opal's other hand shot out and this time the slap he received knocked Rastrow back on his heels.

"I would propose, Marshal Rastrow, that you stow your hostilities," Judge Tabor said in a quiet, even-mannered tone. "This town has seen quite enough violence of late, without you making matters worse."

"I want this Injun nigger jailed," Rastrow said, a note of hysteria having crept into his voice. "You hear me, judge?"

"On what charge?" asked the judge.

"On the charge of . . . striking an officer."

"A foul-mouthed one," Helen Gates said, breaking her silence.

"Need I remind you, sir," put in the judge, "this is not the military."

"Well, resisting arrest, then," Rastrow shot back.

"On what charge are you arresting her?" the judge asked calmly. He was wearing dark, smoked glasses with white frames. His blindness coupled with his highly professional demeanor had a tendency to unnerve Rastrow.

"Obviously she assaulted my deputy,"

Rastrow said. "I know Lefty Price. He would scarcely have come voluntarily."

"What about the dead woman over at Doc Whitelaws's?" Opal Cameron asked.

"Listen, that nigger was the wife of a bank robber. Another one of that same gang killed Noah Pine. Don't tell me that's anything to get all worked up about?"

"Sir," said the judge. "I have heard enough. I propose you resign immediately from the office of marshal."

"What do you say to that, Mr. Rogan?" Rastrow asked, turning toward the banker in what was becoming a desperately serious situation and hardly what he had expected when riding so proudly into town.

"I think his honor is quite justified in his demand," Rogan said, moving forward slightly. "You have apparently fulfilled the assignment the bank gave you, to bring in Ben Massingale. Your services as marshal will no longer be required."

"God damn it, Rogan," Rastrow said, his voice cracking. "You can't do this to me. I just caught Ben Massingale." He turned to the group in the small office at large and slanted his eyes at each of them. "Doesn't that mean anything to you people?"

"What happened to Silas Pine?" Rawina asked, her jaw jutting out.

"Be that as it may, did you find the bank's money, Mr. Rastrow?" Rogan asked.

"No, but I got the man who knows where it's hidden."

"You mean we have him," the judge put in gently.

"Who do you mean by 'we'?" Rastrow demanded.

"This town, Mr. Rastrow," the judge said.

Black Ellis's hand brushed against his gun butt, but this action only caused Santiago Cruz to thrust his pistol barrel more sharply into the man's backbone.

"Don' move, or I weel eshoot," he reminded softly.

"I don't get it," Rastrow said, genuinely bewildered. "I bring in Massingale and I find everyone backing this nig . . . this black Injun here and carrying on about. . . ."

"That will be quite enough," Rogan said. He turned graciously toward Opal. "Would you be so kind, ma'am, as to hold this little one for me? Perhaps even take him from this room. I do not trust my temper at this point."

Opal took Baby Hope delicately in her hands. She had long, tapered fingers. Gage Cameron, who had been to Indian school and liked to read books, had seen a bust of Nefertiti, an ancient Egyptian queen, and as a result he had called Opal his Nubian princess. But there was nothing regal about the way she took the infant from Horace Rogan's outstretched hands. She was Opal Bedoe again, and she began cooing to Baby Hope as she had once cooed to her own baby before evil men had killed her husband and then set fire to the cabin in which Ishmael had been sleeping.

As packed as the room was, everyone made way for Opal as she walked now, carrying Baby Hope, who was silent but whose eyes were open, staring up at Opal's face. Even Black Ellis moved backwards, as far as Santiago's drawn pistol would let him.

"I think we should be going as well," Rawina Pine announced, nodding to Helen and Susan Gates. "But I'll want to know about the end of Silas Pine, Mr. Rastrow, so be sure not to leave town without coming over to the trading post."

"I don't plan on leaving town," Rastrow insisted.

The women filed out of the office into the street. Their departure allowed Reno Poteet and Roy Maginnis to enter the office, supporting Ben Massingale's body between them.

Seeing the injured and staggering Massingale helped restore Rastrow's confidence.

"You, too, Mex. Leave with the women," he addressed Santiago Cruz. "The men of this town have got a little payin' of respect due to me and my men. You ain't wanted."

"*Señor* Joodge? You want for me to leev'?"

"Perhaps that would be best, Santiago," Judge Tabor replied, adjusting his dark-lensed glasses on his nose. "But wait for me outside. I shall want to talk with you."

"*Si*," said Santiago, holstering his weapon as he backed cautiously toward the door. He turned only when he bumped into Hal Owen who was standing in the narrow doorway with the other members of the posse. They parted for him, and he vanished behind them.

"Now, see here, Rogan . . . ," Rastrow began. He didn't get to finish.

"No, now you see here," Rogan broke in on him. "You were hired for a job. You have executed it. If you will accompany me over to the bank, I will see that you are paid the reward I offered for Ben Massingale's capture."

"Father," said Malinda Tabor, speaking for the first time since Rastrow and Ellis had entered the office, "Ben Massingale's been hurt. I think someone should go fetch Doc Whitelaws."

"I already done that, ma'am," Hal Owen said.

Roy Maginnis and Reno Poteet had just eased Massingale down onto the bunk in the cell that had been standing empty. Poteet had seen Lefty Price in the next cell and the two exchanged glances. This did not bode well, Poteet thought.

"Lew," Rogan was saying, "if it's acceptable to you, I propose that we appoint Roy Maginnis Acting Marshal until an election can be held."

"Now, just a damned minute . . . ," Rastrow said.

"I accept your proposal, Horace," Judge Tabor said. "Roy, is it agreeable to you?"

"Anything you say, judge," said the big smithy from inside Massingale's cell.

"Isom," Rogan said, his voice firm, "as I mentioned before, I suggest that we adjourn to the bank."

Rastrow conceded defeat with a shrug.

"Reno," he said, "you and Black wait for me over to the Gold Bar."

"What about Lefty?" Reno asked, stepping out of the Massingale cell.

"Let him be," Rastrow said coldly. "It seems he murdered that Crowley woman."

Reno's glance traveled the room nervously, but he did not speak further. He signaled to Black Ellis and the two walked out the door.

Tip Maginnis, who had been standing patiently just outside the door with Kerry Lu next to him, had heard everything. When

Rogan and Rastrow emerged, the banker in the lead, he whispered to Kerry Lu, "Here's your chance."

Kerry Lu slipped past Tip and rushed into the office and made her way to the cell where her father was lying.

"Dad," she said in a voice strained with anguish. "Dad?"

"I don't rightly think he can hear you, miss," said Roy Maginnis, in a tone surprisingly soft for a man of his girth. "He lost consciousness while we was on the trail and has been in and out, mostly out, ever since."

"But I can stay near him till Doc comes?" Kerry Lu pleaded.

"You surely can," the blacksmith said.

"Roy," said Judge Tabor, who had made sense out of everything he could not see and who appeared to know who had left the room, who had entered, and who had remained, "the child can tend to her pa. I want to swear you in, legally and properly."

Roy Maginnis squeezed Kerry Lu's shoulder gently, smiled down at her, and then moved on past her out of the cell.

Chapter Eighteen

A voice woke him. He didn't seem able to open his eyes.

"I want to cut off the head," the voice was saying.

"We haven't time for that. Just help me pull Massingale out from under this carcass and let's be going."

Pine tried concentrating on opening his eyes. The back of his head ached as if it had been crushed in by a burning rock. His entire back, from his neck across the shoulder blades to the small of it, was alive with livid pain that showed red before his eyes. *If only he could open them!* But the intense pain of being conscious was just too much for him. He began to drift, his ears ringing with the thunder of crashing, cascading water. Was this the place of the trap? Was he done for? These questions occurred to him as he began plunging downward into darkness.

It wasn't until he heard the voice again that consciousness returned. Or had it been the sharp toe of a Justin boot kicking him in the side, just above the area of livid pain, that had brought him around?

"He ain't dead, Isom. Not quite, he ain't."

"Leave him. He's known to be out here. The bear killed him. If he ain't daid by tonight, he soon will be. C'mon, now, climb in the saddle. I want to be on the trail with Massingale before Black and that posse catch up to us."

A wet splotch hit Silas Pine's face. It burned in the open wound on his cheek. He still couldn't open his eyes. Maybe they were crusted shut with dried blood. The wet splotch? It wasn't rain. Perhaps it was tobacco spittle. The gulf began opening once more, the roar returning to his ears, and Silas faded silently into the yawning depths.

He slept.

It was the cold which woke him the next time. The wind had died completely and been replaced by a mantle of frost that gripped and locked his body. The pain from the open lacerations on his back seemed to have subsided in this cold. But he didn't try to move. His eyes were still crusted shut and so he concentrated on opening them. He worked hard at it.

The lashes tore apart as the lids ripped open. He did not move his head but he moved his eyes, probing in all directions. The light was a dismal gray with shadows moving through

171

it. He heard something. It wasn't a voice this time, but loud sniffing. It came from somewhere behind his head. Then more sniffing as padded feet moved around his head. He looked sideways and could see a phantom in the shadows. It continued sniffing him.

Man smell probably. The phantom faded. It was a timber wolf. Of that Silas was certain. He couldn't see it any more, and he couldn't hear it, but he felt it was near. Then he began to doubt even that as he heard snarling and then the sound of slashing teeth off somewhere in the darkness.

Wolves didn't attack men. Yet the sound was the same as wolves tearing and slashing at food, at meat. Massingale? Could he be dead? Were they feasting on his dead meat?

No. He remembered a voice saying they were taking Massingale away. Or had that been a dream? Had he just imagined it?

For no reason except the terror he was beginning to feel, Silas jerked himself as he tried to sit up. It was involuntary. He couldn't help it. He screamed with the coming of the pain, a more terrible pain than he had ever felt before.

There came a sudden alarmed pause in the activity of the phantoms near a great black mound. Off to the side, there was more snarling. He could see smaller mounds.

They must have killed the cubs. Silas was sure of it.

He was silent as he sat there. The wolves began tearing again and eating. He was trying now to recall the way the area had looked in daylight. There was the cave. The spot where Massingale had buried the washers. The burnt out depression where Massingale had once had a fire. The small mountain rivulet beyond the cave. . . .

That was it. Water. Now that he thought about it, he was parched, his tongue swollen in his mouth. If he could only crawl in the direction of the rivulet. He would have to lay back down to do that. He could feel the sensation of blood creeping down his back again, which was almost bare to the cold and frost in the air. That was where the bear had torn at him. The back of his head throbbed.

He tried to lower himself down carefully onto his right side. He had no control. He crashed sideward instead. Pain assailed his right shoulder and then shot out in bright streamers across his entire back. He felt himself slipping again, falling backward into darkness. Was this what his bad dream had meant? Or was his heart failing him? He did seem to be suffocating. He made a motion to stretch out his right arm and the pain became so intense that he lost consciousness.

He slept.

It was the sound of rushing water that woke him. He could hear it and then suddenly he felt it strike his lacerated neck and shoulders and the back of his head. Something had been pulling on his arms, holding his hands. He seemed to remember that, even though he had been unconscious. He had been dragged on his stomach, being pulled forward by his hands and arms.

"Ye maun lie still and brook the grief of it, Mr. Pine," a voice said close to his ear. The hands were holding him now by the sides of his head, keeping his face up out of the water, but he could feel the turbulence, icy cold, almost paralyzing, and yet soothing, as the back of his head seemed to float in the current. "There's naething else to be done. The water will cleanse ye sure."

Silas was incapable of struggle. As the cold penetrated his heated flesh, the pain lessened. His mind, his memory, was returning as with a kaleidoscope of images, of the darkness, the night, the wolves, and before that the outraged she-bear.

"Miz Massingale?" he whispered in surprise and confusion.

"Ay, man, the same, but ye've the right now

to call me Shawn."

Silas could not see her, although he could feel the strength in her fingers as she held delicately yet firmly to his head.

"Ben," he whispered. "You'd best look to him. He's over there. He . . . he may be dead."

"Hush. Don't speak."

He didn't then. He lay back, he couldn't tell for how long, letting the cold water flow beneath and around him. He felt some of it splash his face. His head, held apparently then with only one hand, was being bathed, and his face. Water from a cupped palm dribbled down onto the lower part of his face. He opened his mouth instinctively. The next time the dribbling water came, he drank. He almost inhaled the water, stopped himself. The next time he knew what to do. He drank more cautiously, but he drank.

He was drifting in and out again when the cold began to make him ache in a different way. Shawn's voice came to him.

"D'ye think ye cauld stay here a mite? At least a few minutes so I can get to the cave and start a fire?"

"I can try," Silas rasped.

"I brought some salve and bandages. I thought Ben might be needing them. They'll nae do for ye. Ye've need of a doctor and nae way to get one. But I ken they won't hurt ye and they might help a little."

"Ben? What happened to Ben?"

"They've got him, Mr. Pine. They led him away, tied to a horse. They left ye to die. I saw that much. Ben's pack's still here. But nae a horse. Just mine. I fear we'll taigle many a weary foot, or we get clear! But, can ye rest here? Just a little?"

"If you could just help me get turned over and in the right direction, I'll sure try, Miz Massingale."

She laughed at that. He couldn't see her face, for it was too dark, but the music of her laugh cheered him.

"It's Silas that ye be, then, for I am Shawn."

Before he could answer, Silas heard her rise behind him. She must have been squatting on her haunches in the cold water all this time! One hand gripped his right, held him aloft until the other gripped his left. He was dragged and pulled suddenly to one side, away from the rivulet.

"Roll, now, Silas, and I'll try to turn ye."

He knew what she meant and he rolled. Shooting pains rippled across his back and red flashes appeared before his eyes, but he was on his stomach.

"Ye should nae move 'til I get back."

He said nothing, but he was able to pull

his arms back toward him so he could rest on his elbows.

"Didna ye hear me, Silas?"

"You must be soaking wet," he said.

"Ay, but only below my gunbelt."

"Gunbelt?"

"Ay. I left Kerry Lu with a friend and went to find my man. If it had to be that his bed would be the muircock's and his life that of a hunted deer, then I'd share an empty belly with him and sleep with him with me hand upon a weapon." She paused. "Nae more of this. Ye stay here. I'll go start a fire in the cave. We have need of the warmth."

He saw her silhouette move away from him, dissolve into darkness.

"Wolves," he muttered, but she must not have heard him. Her footsteps sloshed and squished as from wet boots and then there was only the night sounds, the rushing water, the faint hoot of an owl.

By digging in his elbows, Silas found that he could pull himself forward slowly. He worked at it. Maybe he could make the cave if he really tried.

Chapter Nineteen

Horace Rogan lit a harp lamp which stood on the corner of the polished surface of his mahogany desk in his private office. The sky was still overcast, a bleak gray, and the wind had the nip of dampness in it. The light illumined a circle before the desk including the leather chair in which the banker invited former Acting Marshal Rastrow to sit.

"Care for a cigar?" Rogan asked the horse hunter, proffering a polished wooden box containing long nines with a gold name plate on top of it engraved with the initials H.R.

"Nope," Rastrow said and pulled out a bag of North Carolina plug cut that had a draw string the same as Bull Durham smoking tobacco. He fetched out a suitable chunk and placed it in his mouth, tucking it between his lower lip and bottom teeth.

Rogan seated himself in the swivel chair behind the desk and clipped the tip of the long nine with a gold cigar cutter he kept at the other end of his watch chain a few links above the fob. The light was such that it kept him in relative shadow, augmented by the window behind the chair which looked out onto the bleak sky and a dilapidated stable. This light tended to highlight the planes of Rastrow's face, glistening with silver stubble among the short whisker growth from a few days in the saddle without shaving.

"I thought we had a deal, Rogan," Rastrow said, the words arching beneath a suppressed fury.

"You mean about taking over those four repossessed ranches to begin your own spread?" Rogan asked, and puffed a cloud of blue smoke at the flaming match with which he had lit his cigar.

"You know damned well that ain't what I mean. You had no business calling for my resignation from the marshalin' job, 'specially after we just brought in Ben Massingale."

"I don't suppose," Rogan said in a hushed tone, leaning over his desk top, "you managed to retrieve that sack of money Massingale stole from this bank?"

"Not yet we didn't, nor are we likely to get the truth out of him now that I'm not in charge of the prisoner."

Rogan leaned back on his chair, puffed another cloud of smoke toward the ceiling, and chuckled.

"What you think is so funny, Rogan? That picture of you holdin' onto that nigger baby."

Rogan's chuckle was cut short and his eyes became dark and piercing. There was a short pause before he spoke again.

"That 'nigger baby' as you refer to Baby Hope just happens to be an orphan entirely by your doing, Isom, and that is essentially why you were forced out of office."

"I had nothin' to do with that nigger woman's death!"

"Do you expect me, or anyone else in this town, to believe that your man Lefty Price just took it upon himself to club Aurelia Crowley on the head in the Gates's kitchen, load her unconscious body into a wagon, and drive her out to the Crowley place?"

"I ain't sayin' that now."

"I'll go you one better, Isom. If you ever try saying it, no one will believe you."

"I suppose you're takin' the word of that black Injun."

"I don't have to take her word for anything. I have eyes. I can see." Rogan paused long enough to set his cigar down on an ashtray on his desk. He dropped his voice even lower than it had been before. "I also know, Isom, why you had your men kill her."

"What yuh mean, *you know?*"

"My housekeeper, Helen Gates, told me two mornings back that Aurelia Crowley insisted neither Sam nor any of the other men did for

180

Obbie. That's why I went over to the Gates place to see Mrs. Crowley. Your men had already taken her away, although I didn't know that then. But — thank God! — they left Baby Hope behind or, I suppose, she'd be dead by this time, too."

"Listen, I mebbe don't have as much use for darkies as you do, but even I draw the line somewhere, Rogan, and I draw it when it comes to killin' babies."

Rogan leaned forward now as far as he could across the desk and his voice was a harsh whisper.

"I figure, Rastrow, that old Silas Pine and I got one thing in common."

"What's that?" Rastrow asked defensively. He didn't like the course this talk had been taking any more than the course of events since he returned to Grafton and his scowl showed it. "You ain't dead. That's the only thing you an' Pine could have in common."

"I don't think so." Rogan rasped out the words. "We've both lost a son, Mr. Rastrow. Both were shot down by a bullet. And your time is running out to admit it. I saw you that night we flushed Sam Crowley and Ben Massingale out of hiding. I saw you plug the marshal. I didn't have a whole lot of use for him as it was and I could see how he might have stood in the way of the little deal we had between us. But — and this is the point" — his fingers sharply tapped a tattoo on the polished surface of the desk, punctuating his words — "if those four small ranchers who had gone in with Obbie on that planned robbery didn't shoot my son in the back, who does that leave?"

Rastrow flinched in his chair. His cheeks had retained a deep, if dim, redness from where Opal Cameron had slapped him. Now they were flaming.

"You sayin' I did for yore son?"

"You, Isom, or one of your men."

Rastrow laughed nervously. "You're accusin' me of two murders, there, bucko. If you got proof, why did you stop with just gettin' me to resign? Why ain't I sharin' a cell with Lefty Price?"

Rogan leaned back, the hinges of his chair squeaking faintly. It effectively pulled his face completely out of the light now that the sky had darkened somewhat outside. He had taken a blind stab. He hadn't really believed Rastrow was behind Obbie's death, but he had pressed his point because it was to his advantage in what he wanted from the man. "If I could prove you were implicated, you may be assured, I'd have had the county prosecutor swear out a warrant for your arrest and Judge Tabor would now have the case ready for trial."

There was a brass cuspidor situated alongside the leather chair in which Rastrow was sitting. He leaned forward and spit.

"Then it's kind of a Mexican standoff, huh?" he asked, leaning back again, but this time with his right hand much closer to his holstered Colt.

"Not quite," Rogan stated emphatically. "You got together that ten thousand dollars to complete your downpayment on those four homesteads?"

"I'm workin' on it."

"I am afraid that is not good enough, Mr. Rastrow. Your continued presence in this town is very dangerous from your point of view and from the bank's as well. As I say, I can understand your killing Marshal Pine. He was too honest for his own good. If you hadn't plugged him, somebody else would've sooner or later. I am less certain about poor Obbie. I have had a lot of time over the last two days to think it all out. If Obbie had succeeded with that fool robbery, I wouldn't have seen him again. Even as it was, with my having got wise to what he was planning and placing you and your men in the bank the day of the robbery, had he lived, he'd probably have headed out anyway, penniless. My wife doesn't see it the way I do, but I lost our son some years back."

Rastrow was rarely surprised by anything in life. He had lived long enough, and seen enough, that he felt he pretty well knew how people would react and what they might do. But this attitude in Horace Rogan genuinely surprised him.

"You writin' him off like a bad debt, or sumthin'?" he asked, his tone indicating none of what he felt privately about the banker's coldness.

"After a manner of speaking, Mr. Rastrow, that is precisely what I'm doing. And there's more. I'm writing *you* off as a bad debt."

"Me?"

"That's right. Your man Lefty hasn't talked yet, but I'm sure, given time and the hopelessness of his situation, he will tell what happened. When he does, there will be evidence of murder against you and, believe me, the warrant won't be long behind."

"I didn't kill that nigger woman."

"No, *you* didn't. But it was done on your orders, I'm sure. That makes you just as guilty in the eyes of the law as the man who may have actually done the deed."

"Listen, Reno was told to tap her gently so we could hustle her out of town. That's all. He must of hit her too hard."

"Much too hard, Mr. Rastrow. Hard

184

enough to kill her. Doc Whitelaws examined the body when Opal Cameron brought Mrs. Crowley into town. He says she died of severe concussion and shock. However it happened, all deals are off as of this moment. I suggest you and your men clear out tonight, while you still can."

"And what about Price? I suppose we're s'posed just to leave him sit in that cell 'til he decides to sing?"

"Not at all. I suggest you take him with you."

"An' how're we s'posed to do that with the new marshal you got and the guards that'll be 'round that jail now that Massingale's back."

"Ben Massingale does not seem to be in very good shape."

"If he were, yuh think I'da brought him back without gettin' the loot first? I figgered on working on him here in town."

Rogan leaned over and opened his top right-hand drawer. By almost reflex action, Isom Rastrow had his Colt half drawn when he saw the banker's hands move forward into the pool of light from the lamp.

"I am not about to pull a gun on you, Mr. Rastrow," Rogan assured him. Rastrow let his pistol slide back into its holster, but he leaned forward in the deep chair so he could see the

185

pile of greenbacks the banker was holding. "There's two thousand five hundred dollars here."

"Yuh said a thousand for Massingale, dead or alive."

"No, Mr. Rastrow, I said a thousand dollars for the man who got him. I meant I wanted him dead. He isn't dead, Isom."

"He ain't alive by much."

"Possibly not, but he *is* alive."

"You want me and the boys to plant him, is that it?"

"Not exactly," the banker said, a suaveness entering his voice now. "I will arrange it so you can get your man Price out of the jail. I don't know if Doc will decide to treat Massingale in his cell or have him taken to the one-room hospital which is attached to his office and home. No matter. I want Massingale taken out of town with you."

"You want him just dumped on the trail, if he dies?"

"Not *if* he dies. He is to die. I am paying you fifteen hundred dollars to see that he does die and that his body is never found."

Rastrow sank back into the cushions of the leather chair, his forehead knotted in perplexity. One rope-burned, roughened hand came up and made scratching sounds as he rubbed his stubbled beard.

186

"And the horse ranch?"

"Gone, Mr. Rastrow. I am afraid Reno Poteet has made it impossible for either of us to think further about that little transaction. It is not that the Crowley woman herself was so important. But there is Baby Hope. I have arranged for Opal Cameron to stay temporarily at my home and tend to the child. She lost her own baby some time back and she wants to raise Baby Hope with her husband's people. I figure she'll pull out as soon as she finds out what Lefty Price knows."

"She ain't gonna find out nothin' if we take Lefty with us."

"That's right, Mr. Rastrow." Rogan had left the stack of greenbacks in the center of his desk, neatly stacked just in front of the ink well and pen buried in buckshot. He now picked up his cigar, struck another match, and touched the tip with the flame, puffing intently. "We've all had to cut our losses on this deal, probably me more than you and your men. I'm stuck with four homesteads that aren't worth a whole lot and I've lost my only son. You've lost your hope for a horse ranch and a lawman's job that was to be temporary anyway. You take this money, and do what I have asked, and I'll do my best to see that the whole thing is forgotten. Silas Pine was the only one keeping the question of Noah's death open, and you say he's dead in the Neversummers."

"Yeah, a she-bear got him an' Massingale. I didn't put a bullet in the old man. No need. It feels like snow up there. He'll be frozen by tonight and, when his body is found, the only marks there'll be on it if the scavengers leave sumthin' behind will be those of that grizzly. I never saw a man so filled with blood as Pine was. That bear really gave him a workin' over."

"Then," Horace Rogan said, leaning forward in his swivel chair once more, "you have only to reach out and pick up this money. If you agree to my terms about Massingale, you'll have your man back and twenty-five hundred dollars for your trouble."

"You seem ta be fergittin' one thing, Rogan. A little matter of the bank's money. If Massingale's dead, how're you ever going to recover it?"

Rogan puffed quietly on his cigar for a few moments. "Like I said to you earlier, we have to cut our losses on this one, Mr. Rastrow. And you're right. The bank stands to lose a whole lot more than you do."

Had this conversation occurred a week ago, Rastrow wouldn't have allowed Rogan to put him off this way. He was certain now, more certain than he had ever been before, that there was something wrong with the way Rogan wanted Ben Massingale dead. What if everyone was wrong and the small rancher hadn't really taken the bank's money? He fully intended to live up to his side of the bargain, if it meant getting Lefty Price out of jail and killing Massingale. That was easily done. He knew just the spot, about two hundred miles away. Twin Falls. A body thrown over the edge there would never be found. But once he had Massingale, he wasn't going to see him killed until he knew for sure that he didn't know where the money was. And if Massingale didn't, his body would get tossed all right, but Isom'd be coming back to town for one more short talk with Horace Rogan.

Rastrow rose from the leather chair, reached out, and picked up the wad of greenbacks.

"Now, s'pose, Mr. Rogan, you tell me just how you figger we should go about gettin' Lefty and Massingale."

189

Chapter Twenty

Snow had begun gently to fall. The wind had died down to almost nothing. If it were to return, there was a good possibility of a blizzard with major drifting. Shawn Massingale had found sufficient kindling in the cave to light a fire with a phosphorus match from the block of them she carried wrapped in oilskin and she had added to the small flame some of the still partially dry wood Ben had obviously cut and set aside for his own camp fire.

She had led the roan mare inside the cave despite more than a little resistance at the strong bear smell. She tied Chooky to a heavy but narrow rock which had fallen from a wall and then undid the tie strings behind the cantle which held her Navajo rug in place. She spread the rug near the fire. The sheepskin coat she was wearing kept her relatively warm.

It had not been snowing at all when she had left Silas Pine near the mountain stream and it was so dark now it was difficult to find her way. Smaller furred beasts, coyotes she guessed, had joined the ravenous wolves. There was only occasional snarling or a teeth-gnashing growl. But she could make out a gray coat here and there from the dim, flickering light emitted from the cave.

She walked slowly in the direction she had come after leaving Pine, allowing her eyes a chance to adjust to the enveloping gloom now wrapped in a damp curtain of large snowflakes that clung to her face and adhered to her clothes.

It was the sound of the flowing stream which told her she must be near to where she had left Noah's pa, but it wasn't until she tripped over his prostrate body that she fell to her knees to make certain he was still alive. Pine was breathing deeply, his face awash with sweat, his skin hot to her touch. He was unconscious and obviously feverish.

She didn't think she would be up to dragging him back to the cave. It had been difficult enough to drag him to the stream earlier.

She hurried back to the cave to fetch the rawhide reata she carried on the saddle and to lead Chooky through the falling snow by her reins. As resistant as Chooky had been about entering the cave, she seemed no less reluctant now to leave it and only after several determined jerks was Shawn able to get her to follow.

Finding Silas the second time was less difficult than the first, although she didn't know why this was so, since visibility was so poor she had no real landmarks to follow or even her footsteps in the accumulating snow. Shawn had to be certain that Pine would not roll over onto his lacerated back, neck and head. After desperately pondering where to attach the riata, she decided to tie it around his feet. She had left the Navajo rug in the cave but had not yet undone her bedroll. Dumping the foodstuffs she had brought onto the ground, she packed the bandages, salve, and the small bottle of carbolic acid into the voluminous pockets of her sheepskin coat.

Laying the blanket down on the ground, using her hands and her sense of touch to tell her what she was doing, she kept one end of the riata tied to the horn. It would give her some control over Chooky if she decided to bolt back toward the cave or became spooked by the wolves and coyotes. The other end of the riata she looped a few times around her left arm.

She had literally to drag Silas Pine by his feet until his body was on the blanket. It meant turning him around completely and the act nearly exhausted her reserve of strength. Her fingers were cold and stiff as she fastened the riata around the edge of the blanket and around Pine's boots, making sure to snug it sufficiently that the blanket would remain and his boots not slip from his feet.

It was slow going, that trek back to the cave. Time and distance were to be measured in long minutes. Twice she halted the roan to make sure the riata was still securely tied to Pine.

Approaching the mouth of the cave at last, Chooky seemed more stubborn than ever about entering it a second time. It took considerable coaxing and finally a hard slap on her stiffened neck before the animal would budge. When she began once more to move, it was too fast. By the time Chooky was again inside the cave, the blanket and Silas's boots had worked loose. The blanket was at the cave's mouth. The boots still dangled at the end of the riata.

With an oath in her frustration, Shawn tied the roan mare to the same narrow rock. There was nothing else for it. She would have to tug and pull the unconscious and feverish man the rest of the way into the cave.

Shawn slipped twice on the hard-rock floor of the cave, once falling hard on her bottom, before she had the man placed on the Navajo rug. Her arms and legs were trembling as she stooped to assure herself that he was still alive.

Pine was still breathing. He seemed restless. Shawn got out the carbolic acid and the salve and applied them as best she could to the exposed tissues. She had to use her pocket knife to cut away what was left of his coat and shirt, both of which were in tatters, the material adhering to the coagulated and congealing blood. That he was alive at all seemed little short of a miracle to her.

Before trying to bandage his wounds, Shawn made her way back into the darkness for a last time to retrieve the foodstuffs she had left behind. Snow was still falling in large wet flakes but, mercifully, there was little wind. Maybe it would stay that way until daylight.

Until daylight, Shawn thought to herself. *And then what?*

It was this thought which preoccupied her all the way back to the cave and even while she piled more wood on the fire and began the bandaging process. She recalled when she had first come upon this spot that Ben's camping gear had been left behind by the lawmen.

Once she had Silas bandaged as well as she could, having bound the bandaging round and round his torso, having to lift his upper body slightly as she did so, she breathed a long sigh. Then it was back out into the night and the snow to locate Ben's camp implements and his foodstuffs. Fortunately, he had camped some distance away from the cave and from the carcasses of the bears. None of the animals still congregated around or near the bodies had bothered to investigate. However, locating the exact campsite in the darkness and falling snow was quite as harrowing and time-consuming as locating Silas Pine earlier.

There was no way to tell how much time elapsed, but Shawn figured it must have taken her a good hour to locate Ben's camp gear and fetch it to the cave. He had a side of bacon. She cut generous strips of this and placed them in the fry pan. He also had a small sack of ground coffee and a tin pot in which this could be heated. Not wanting to venture back through the snow and darkness another time to the mountain stream to get water, she went out and collected snow in the tin pot until she had enough to make two cups of coffee. She had packed herself a half loaf of bread, dried out by this time, but moistened it with bacon grease.

Silas Pine had not regained consciousness at any point since she had gone back for him, only now his restlessness seemed greater. His big body seemed to be trembling with racking chills even with the fire nearby, the Navajo rug beneath him, and the bedroll blanket spread out on top of him.

Shawn unsaddled Chooky, rubbed her down as best she could, and then brought both saddle and saddle blanket to the fire. She set the saddle blanket on the far side of Pine's body, away from the fire. It was here she sat, staring down at the man she had once so feared for Ben's sake and to whom she was profoundly grateful for what he had done that day she and Kerry Lu had been attacked by Reno Poteet and Bruno Banes.

There had been only one sack of Bull Durham left at the place and she had carried this and a packet of papers in a shirt pocket for Ben. During long winter nights at the cabin, after Kerry Lu had gone to bed, Ben had taught her how to roll a cigarette. Occasionally Shawn would join him in smoking one. No one knew, of course. Certainly Helen Gates or Rawina Pine, had they known, would have been as shocked as they would be now if they could see Shawn Massingale, her knees drawn up before her, sitting beside Silas Pine wearing pants!

Shawn opined she had it coming after all she had been through, so she rolled herself a cigarette and smoked it down, just sitting there, watching Pine breathe, sipping the last of her coffee, filtering the dregs of the grounds with her very strong white teeth. Most frontier women did not have teeth like Shawn's. Good stock is how she accounted for it. Her daddy had been a seafaring man, a Scotsman. He had wanted a boy. He had had the name all picked out. It was to be Sean, a name especially fond to her Irish mother whose favorite uncle had that name. Only the red-headed baby, with more hair than any respectable baby was supposed to have at birth, turned out to be a girl.

After she had made her way alone to the States, Shawn had phonetically Anglicized her name. Her daddy had died at sea and not long after, when she was eighteen, her mother's life had been claimed by pneumonia.

Pine's chills, if anything, seemed worse than before. Adding more fuel to the fire, Shawn returned to the saddle blanket and slipped out of the sheepskin coat. Spreading the coat over the two of them, she wormed her way closer to Pine, burrowing under the blanket which covered him. Turning him slightly so that one arm was over her shoulder, she pressed her buttocks against his groin. His shivering seemed to subside for a time.

Shawn was suddenly very tired. Without wanting to sleep, she couldn't help herself but drifted off, with the sound of Silas Pine's heavy breathing in her left ear. The regular deep inhalations and exhalations were somehow comforting to her. The snow effectively cut off the sounds from outside and Chooky was quiet, probably dozing, dreaming whatever it is that horses dream.

Later, when Shawn awoke, noticing that the fire had burned down, she was divided at first if she should make the effort to get up from her warm spot to attend to it. Silas Pine was hot and sweating. He had made her both damp and warm.

Feeling his male member erect against her left buttock is what made up Shawn Massingale's mind for her. She pulled away, slowly letting Silas Pine down flat on his stomach.

Standing up beside the man, certain that he was still unconscious, she remarked aloud, knowing no one could hear her, "I'll tell ye this at the start, Silas Pine, for it is something I ken well. Asked aboot your chances when I found ye, I'd have said: Nane. But if ye can still become hard as a bone, ay, it's a well man ye'll be if I can but get ye to Adakhai."

Her face burned as she said it, but it was both shock and puzzlement that silenced her, not embarrassment. She could not tell why she had uttered that name, or had had such a thought, but having said it aloud, she knew it was true. She was convinced, as if witness to a revelation, that the one thing that would save Silas Pine's life, and perhaps that of her Ben, was to be found at the old Navajo's encampment. She now had her answer.

"At daylight," she whispered, leaning forward, her body trembling but not just from the sudden contact of chilled air with her sweaty clothes, "we shall go to Adakhai."

Chapter Twenty-One

Isom Rastrow had been angry as he had trudged along the boardwalk toward the Gold Bar Saloon to meet up with Reno Poteet and Black Ellis. Everything that could possibly have gone wrong since he and his horse-hunting crew had arrived in Grafton, it seemed to him, had gone wrong. Instead of ending up with a horse ranch comprised of an entire section of deeded land and ten thousand to the good, two men had been killed, three if you counted Silas Pine, and a nester woman. Six men, if you counted the three men shot down as a result of the bank robbery. And for a payoff, he had only a niggardly twenty-five hundred in greenbacks to show for it. That was a lot of killing for so little.

He was not sure how it had been done, but Horace Rogan had successfully played him for a dupe. To Rastrow it all came to one overwhelming conclusion. If he couldn't have the horse ranch in the Neversummer range he had wanted, he wasn't leaving until he had the money to buy one somewhere else.

The time had come to copper all his bets.

He simply was not going to play any longer according to Rogan's rules. He was going to call for a new deck and now, for a change, he would be dealing.

Poteet and Ellis were drinking sullenly at a table near the back of the spacious barroom when Rastrow entered. Joining them, waving to one side their expressions of curious inquiry, Rastrow called for a new bottle and glasses. Once they were served by the barkeep, they were relatively isolated in the back of the saloon. It was late in the afternoon and too early for the early evening crowd to begin their inevitable arrival. Even the gaming tables were idle except for a single poker game at a table near the front doors. It was then that Rastrow laid out his plans for that night after they went to supper at a small cafe up the street.

Black Ellis had been charged with getting a wagon from the Grafton Livery Stable and Feed Barn. Ironically, it turned out to be the same wagon that had been used to transport Aurelia Crowley back to her shack. Opal Cameron had used it to bring the dead woman and Lefty Price to Grafton.

Tip Maginnis was on duty at the stable while Santiago Cruz had gone home to supper. If Cruz had been there, Ellis was of a mind to rush things and give him a pistol-whipping on the spot he would remember for a long time to come. As it was, that would have to wait, but not for long.

It struck Ellis that the kid acted suspicious but, if he was, he still didn't ask a direct question. Instead he told of how he had been sent by his father to the Chinaman's to fetch supper for the prisoner. Black remembered seeing the kid leaving Wong Fu's as the three of them were walking up the street to the place after leaving the Gold Bar. Tip made a point of assuring Ellis that at least Lefty Price was being well fed.

Before departing, Ellis flipped the kid a dime for helping him harness the team. Tip must have good eyes. In the lamp glare coming from the big gasoline lamp above the open double doors of the barn, he was able to see the shine of the coin well enough to grab it with the darting suddenness of a toad catching a fly.

Ellis was no fool. He knew the kid would report his renting the wagon to Cruz just as soon as the man returned. Only now that probably would not happen. Cruz's cabin was to be their second stop.

To throw off the kid, or anyone else who might observe his driving out of the stable with the wagon, Ellis headed down the main street in the direction of Rawina Pine's trading post. It was two doors down from the Grafton jail on the other side of the street. Isom Rastrow would already have been there with Reno ordering the supplies they intended to transport to what the men were describing as the temporary camp they were supposed to set up at the place in the Neversummers where Silas Pine had been killed and the grizzly bear shot. They had not had time to give the marshal's father a proper burial. They would attend to that now. It sounded logical, even generous. They would remain near at hand, pending Lefty Price's trial for murder, in case they were needed for any reason. In the meantime, since Isom and Reno knew the exact location and no one else did, they'd be doing what they could for a man who had lost his life trying to bring in the murderer of his son.

Rawina Pine, her iron gray hair still worn in a severe bun at the back of her head and wearing a dark gray dress, was off in one corner of the trading post talking to Rastrow when Ellis opened the heavy wooden door and let himself in after tying the lines to the hitching ring on the loading ramp at the side. The woman's face was pinched, with a slight pallor, evident in the dim light which came from a wall lamp nearby. She and Rastrow were on that side of the large room where the tables of blankets, sougans, and other camping gear were located. Along the back wall and up the opposite side of the room to the small window fronting on the street was a wooden counter. Susan Gates was piling up their order from the various shelves located behind the right-angled counter as Reno Poteet checked the items off the list he held in his hand with the small stub of a pencil.

Rastrow signed with his head to Black Ellis and he joined them.

"I was just tellin' Miz Pine here that old Pine went fast once that bear laid into him," Rastrow said. There was no doubt he wanted Ellis to back him up.

"That's right, ma'am. Why, that griz must have been ten feet tall, astandin' up the way she was. She swiped him a few times and that was it fer him. That's what I heard tell of later. I was with the posse, you recall. Isom here, and Reno, was the ones that did for the she-bear."

Bitterness had caused deep creases to form in the folds between Rawina Pine's nose and her mouth. Her dark eyes were made all the darker and unfathomable by the heavy bluish marks beneath them.

"Couldn't you stop the bear before she killed Silas?" she asked, her tone earnest, as she focused all her attention again on Rastrow.

"We surely tried, Miz Pine. We poured load

after load into that bear. It was some right smart shootin' 'cause we didn't want to hit your . . . the marshal's father. But then he was down and that bear, she turned on us. When she finally did drop, I figger Reno was as surprised as I was, we'd shot her so many times and hadn't stopped her."

"But why?" she asked, perplexed. "Bears usually don't attack people."

"They do, Miz Pine, when they's been shot at," Rastrow said. "That's what we figger happened. Massingale was hidin' out there near where that bear had a cave. Probably opined she'd give him a warning if anyone came near. Pine must of come on Massingale. Tried to shoot him. The bear got worried about its cubs. There were a couple of them. We shot 'em after the she-bear went down. Old Silas, why he must of taken a shot at that bear and it wasn't enough to stop her."

"No, reckon not," she conceded in a small voice. Her eyes glanced for a moment at the puncheon floor and then rose again to meet Isom Rastrow's gaze. "Did you bury him?"

The words, almost whispered, hung in the air. Rastrow shook his head.

"Didn't have time, Miz Pine. We could see Pine was gone but Massingale wasn't. We wanted to get him back to town as soon as we could."

"Then . . . ," she began and paused. "You just left him out there like . . . like carrion."

"Well, not the way you put it, Miz Pine." Rastrow's discomfort was obvious. "Wouldn't worry 'bout it too much. Wolves an' coyotes would be more likely to go after bear meat, if they were to come sniffin' around. Tell you what, though. I've already promised Mr. Rogan and he's told Judge Tabor, that we're setting out tonight in the dark, back into the Neversummers. We can get a couple hours in tonight and, after stopping to set up camp, should be able to start out again at first light and make it to the spot by the early afternoon. We'll bury him, Miz Pine, never fear."

"How would you like to get a discount on that grub your man is buying?" she asked, so suddenly changing the subject that Rastrow was mildly taken aback.

"How so?"

"I'll discount it . . . ," she paused, thinking for a moment, "ten percent, no twenty, if instead of burying him up there, if you'll bring his body back here to town so he can have a proper burial." Her tone, when bargaining, was hard, but the expression on that pinched and pallid face was almost gentle. "I . . . I would like to bury him beside our son, Noah."

"That's right decent of you, Miz Pine, an' it's fitting at that," Rastrow agreed. "Howsomeever, you needn't give us any discount atall. Mr. Rogan told us that he was willin' to pick up the tab fer this himself."

"Horace Rogan!" Rawina said. "What was Silas ever to him?"

"Don't rightly know," Rastrow admitted, "but he also lost a son at the end of Massingale's gun."

Although she had been subliminally aware of it, the thought that, yes, Obbie Rogan had also died, only struck Rawina fully now that Isom Rastrow had reminded her of it. Her emaciated hands fluttered nervously before she excused herself and hurried to help Susan behind the counter.

Rastrow's face said nothing, but there was a small grin playing around the corners of Ellis's wide mouth, visible only to the other man because of where he was standing.

Rastrow waited until the two boxes of grub, extra blankets, and other items had been loaded into the wagon and they had pulled out from the trading post, heading down the alley behind the main street buildings, before he permitted himself a chuckle. He liked the way this was going.

Doc Whitelaws's house was over one street but it backed on this same alley about ten city lots down from the Pine trading post. Rawina Pine and the Gates girl had said they had some inventory to restock and then they would be closing up for the night. Just before Rastrow had climbed into the saddle, the Pine woman had placed a hand on his arm and murmured her gratitude for what he was doing. It only confirmed in Isom Rastrow's mind that there was no telling about women. Here was one who carried the stigma of divorce and yet was concerned about where the man from whom she had parted was going to be buried. It was that, even more than the irony of sticking Rogan with the bill, that had prompted Rastrow to chuckle.

Black Ellis, his horse tied to the tailgate of the wagon, pulled up the team in the alley behind the doctor's house. Rogan had assured Rastrow that he would see to it that the medico was not around provided they arrived at seven. Rastrow had checked his watch at the trading post just before pulling out and it had been almost seven. There was no light from the house except from the rear window of a room that had obviously been added on after the four room, square house had been built. It was this room which was used as the hospital.

Poteet was sent around to the front where he was to enter as quietly as he could. Rastrow would let himself in through the dark kitchen by the back door which opened onto a narrow rear porch. Whitelaws was a bachelor. He didn't have a regular nurse, depending instead on a number of volunteers among the women of the town.

Rastrow had no idea if a volunteer would be on duty tonight and so he was surprised when he and Reno met in the hallway outside the lighted side-room and he saw not only Kerry Lu sitting beside the bed on which Ben Massingale was apparently sleeping but a much older woman wringing out a compress over a pan of water set on a small table near the head of the bed on the right side. The light came from a kerosene lamp turned low on a round table in front of the rear window.

He and Poteet exchanged glances and then drew their guns. The sound seemed to startle the women. The older one turned her head quickly. Kerry Lu just raised her right arm before her mouth which was opening to scream but no sound came. Her eyes held only terror. The eyes of the older, short, sad-faced woman, at once elegantly and drably dressed, seemed more nonplused, even curious, than afraid.

"What do you men want?" she hissed, dropping the cloth she had been holding into the pan of water.

"Who're you?" Poteet breathed.

"I'm Sarah Rogan, and the young lady here

208

is Kerry Lu Massingale." She saw now the expression of fear on Kerry Lu's face and her eyes darted back and forth between the two men.

"Easy," said Poteet, stepping further into the room. "You make a sound and I'll club you with this gun."

"How dare you?" Mrs. Rogan asked.

"I'd listen to him, if I were you," Rastrow said, also entering the room and approaching the bed. "Last woman he hit with that gun, that nigger nester, is daid."

Sarah Rogan drew in her breath sharply but said no more.

"You'll not touch my father again!" Kerry Lu said, rising from the hardwood chair on which she had been seated.

"I'll plug him right while he's laying there if you don't shut up," Poteet said, pulling a length of cord from his coat pocket.

"If you do what you're told and don't try anything, no one will get hurt," Rastrow said, reaching forward and turning Sarah Rogan around so she was facing the bed. "I'll be handin' yuh yer coats and yuh jest put 'em on. As soon as you've done that, Reno'll tie yuh up."

Once they had their coats on, Poteet worked quickly, as if he were wielding a piggin' string. After he tied the wrists of each of the women, he gagged them with strips of sheeting he tore from an empty hospital bed. Rastrow in the meantime hunted up every blanket he could find and took them outside to spread in the wagon bed.

Then the women were taken out to the wagon and forced to climb inside. Rastrow and Poteet went back to get Ben Massingale while Black, his gun drawn, kept his eye on the prisoners. Massingale was rolled over on the hospital bed, the jarring movement bringing him vaguely out of his deep sleep. His hands, too, were bound behind him and he was gagged before he was carried out and put in the wagon on top of some of the blankets.

Among the supplies they had acquired at the trading post was a canvas cover for the wagon bed. The women were told to roll on their sides as Rastrow and Poteet stretched out the canvas over the top of the flat bed and fastened it with tie-strings threaded through small brass holes along the edges of the canvas and secured it to partially rusted sidehooks mounted along the wagon's sides.

"What about that greaser?" Ellis whispered to Rastrow as the man came forward to fasten the last tie-string alongside the front seat.

"What about him?"

"I've got a score to settle with him."

"Some other time, Black. We got Massingale and his kid in one haul. The jail is our next and last stop."

"Who's the old lady?"

"Rogan's wife."

"Why her?"

Rastrow finished and leaned back on the heels of his Justins, peering up at the man in the darkness.

"To keep old Horace company," Poteet put in, finishing up on the other side, and then laughed under his breath.

"Get mounted, Reno," Rastrow said, heading for where his horse was tied. "We've got no time to spare."

Chapter Twenty-Two

Although the closing time weekdays at the Grafton Bank was three o'clock in the afternoon, customarily Horace Rogan, his chief cashier and bookkeeper, the two tellers, and the office clerk worked until five. It was the same weekday mornings. While the bank did not open to the public until ten o'clock, the work day for bank employees began promptly at eight.

It was after five and already dark, with a harsh, wet wind blowing down from the Neversummers, when Rogan entered the picket fence gate of his home and climbed the front steps. In the front hall, he placed his hat on a vacant hook on the combination chair that had a trunk beneath the seat and a mirror mounted in the backboard. The hooks ran along both sides of the mirror.

Rogan suspected that Sarah was not at home because the black-plumed hat she had insisted on wearing whenever she went out since Obbie's death was absent as well as her black shawl. The wall lamp in the hall was lit and spread a faint yellow glimmer which magnified the shadows in corners. The top of the stairs leading to the second floor was enveloped in darkness.

The banker went straight down the hall which connected at the back with the kitchen. He could hear voices as he came closer. Upon entering through the swinging door mounted on well oiled hinges, Rogan found Opal Cameron seated at the square kitchen table, holding Baby Hope cradled in her arms. Although it might have struck a stranger as incongruent for a woman dressed as Opal was to be cooing to a baby, that is precisely what she was doing. The head *banda* was in place and she was wearing her six-gun. Helen Gates was busy at the stove. Both women looked up as Horace came in, the swinging door whooshing closed behind him.

"Mrs. Rogan has gone down to Doc Whitelaws's office," Mrs. Gates said, wiping her hands on her apron and smiling. Responding then quickly to the dark look on the banker's face, she hastened to add, "It's doin' her good to work there as a volunteer now and again when her spirits are low. She is always in much better spirits when she returns. She told me tonight not to hold dinner because she wanted especially to see if Ben Massingale is able to talk about what happened that morning at the bank."

Somehow, to Helen Gates's consternation, these words seemed of little comfort to Horace Rogan. He said nothing but the lines in his face were deeper and his eyes had become anxious.

"I want to thank you for all you've done for Baby Hope and for me," Opal Cameron said, rising from the straight-backed chair on which she had been sitting. "I know it's dark and not a good time to travel, but I sense snow is coming. It will be best for Baby Hope and me if we set out for Adakhai's camp now. Otherwise we may get snowed in, if not here in Grafton, then in the lower passes of the mountains."

What she said distracted Rogan. His dark mood vanished as he approached her.

"I understand how you feel," he said. "But, if you must leave, and on such a windy night as this, may I just sit here a few moments and hold Baby Hope?"

"You surely may," Opal said, holding out the baby to the banker. From her bright eyes and the gurgling sounds of pleasure she made it was obvious Baby Hope recognized Horace Rogan as someone she loved and trusted from the many hours they had been together since he had first found her alone in the Gates's cottage.

Rogan, accepting the baby, held her up high

over his head, smiling unabashedly, and she squeaked with pleasure. Then he began taking her on a tour of the room, swinging her gently in his arms.

"I've fixed you a little packet of food," Helen Gates was saying to Opal. "It's in the pantry. Some cold roast beef sandwiches for you and a small canteen of goat's milk for Baby Hope."

Opal followed the housekeeper into the pantry which opened off the kitchen and led to the dining room beyond. Here a single kerosene lamp in a wall bracket offered what illumination there was to be had.

"Now don't take this wrong, Opal," Mrs. Gates said once they were in the pantry. "I have never asked you about it, but you're leaving and I cannot help saying how well you speak compared to dear Aurelia. It was almost as if you had a white man's education."

"Aurelia was a field slave," Opal said simply. "She came from the deep South. After the War of the Rebellion, she met Sam Crowley in Memphis and they came West to homestead. I had a different experience. I was a house slave to a Cherokee family in the Nations. I was nanny to their two girls when I was only ten. I was tutored right along with them. It was a dangerous thing for the master to have done because it was against the law to educate a slave, even to teach one how to read. But he did it anyway. They were Injuns who had been uprooted and moved a thousand miles by the government to the Nations, but they considered themselves as civilized as any white man. Growing up I learned to read both English and Cherokee.

"My first husband also came from the Nations. He wasn't educated when we first met, but I did teach him enough so he could read a newspaper and even the Bible. We homesteaded just the way Aurelia and Sam did, and my man was killed, too, by white men. Only in his case he hadn't committed any robbery. His only crime was homesteading where a big rancher didn't want anyone, especially anyone of color, squatting on land he considered his by right of having been there first."

"Yes, I know that part of your life," Helen Gates said very softly. "It must have been hard on you, losing your baby that way."

"It wasn't a whole lot better marrying a half breed," Opal said, a smile visible in the dim light because of her very white teeth, "even if he was a rich one by white man's standards. That's why we went back to live with Gage's people, those from his mother's side. His father was from Scotland originally. He and Gage's brother and sister told us we were crazy to do it, but it was what Gage wanted and

I have come to love it at old Adakhai's camp. Gage's people are *Dineh,* not Cherokee. They don't live in houses the way my master and his family did. But there is much to be said for a hogan. And there's more than that. Adakhai is the wisest and kindest man I have ever known. He knows the future. He can paint it with colored sand or show it to you in the light of his sacred fire. It was because Adakhai showed me a vision of Baby Hope in trouble that I came that day to the Crowley place."

"I'm not sure I can agree with you on that, Opal," Helen Gates said. "I do not believe it is given to human beings to know the future. Only God knows what will happen because all that happens was already determined by Him at the very beginning of time. To us God's will remains a mystery. When something terrible happens, such as the death of Master Obbie, we do not know why he died, only that it was God's will. Nothing happens that God has not foreseen and willed it to be so."

Opal Cameron's smile broadened as she looked at the older woman.

"What you are saying is not so different from what I told you I have experienced living with Adakhai who is a shaman of the *Dineh.* If God willed all that will happen even before

217

there was anything, then why wouldn't it be possible for us to see what it was that He willed, provided we found a way that we could see it? That is how it is for Adakhai. The gods control all that happens, but what will happen can be foreseen by certain fortunate ones. Adakhai is such a one."

"It sounds all right the way you put it," Helen Gates said reaching out for the canvas sack with the sandwiches, "but somehow it seems blasphemous. I can't help it. It's just the way I was raised to believe."

Opal took the proffered sack and the canteen and the two women returned in silence to the kitchen. Horace Rogan was now sitting on the same straight-backed chair Opal had occupied. Baby Hope was grabbing onto his right index finger every time he tried to tickle her with it.

"Sorry, Mr. Rogan, but it's time we were leaving," Opal said. "My horse is saddled and waiting out back by your stable."

Reluctantly, Rogan rose. He held Baby Hope close to him, kissed her on one of her milk cheeks and, when he handed her to Opal, there were tears welling up in his eyes.

"You will bring her to visit often?" he asked, his voice a gruff croak.

"I surely will," Opal promised.

To Helen Gates's dismay, the banker told

her that he didn't feel much like eating alone again that night. He would grab a bite at the hotel dining room after he walked Opal and Baby Hope out to the waiting horse.

"And what of the stew I've had simmering for the last couple of hours?" the housekeeper asked.

"Take it home. Susan will be getting home shortly from the trading post. Tell her it's a surprise . . . on me!"

Rogan held Baby Hope as Opal mounted her horse. It was very dark and he could not see very well in the dismal light emanating from the kitchen window and the glass square in the back door leading out onto a small porch stoop. But Opal's capable hands reached out and lifted the infant aloft and then snuggled her partially under the poncho the woman had slipped into before leaving the house.

He stood there listening to the clipclop of retreating hoofbeats before they vanished into the damp wind and the darkness. Then he shuddered. He had not gone back to fetch his hat before coming outdoors and, now, he had no desire to go back into the house. It was strange and, later, he never knew from whence the feeling came, but he was possessed suddenly by a tremendous sadness. All of his planning seemed to have come to nothing and he felt an unaccountable emptiness.

Sarah was at Doc Whitelaws's house! Would she be there when Isom and the others came to get Massingale? He felt he should be anxious about her welfare, and instead he was only indifferent. If everything went the way he intended, Massingale would be dead and his body never found. Rastrow and his wretched crew would be out of his life forever, and good riddance. The money would be his and the bank robbery would begin to fade in the memories of the people in Grafton. Shawn Massingale was said to have gone off into the Neversummers in pursuit of her outlaw husband. She hadn't shown up and just as well. The bank was now in possession of an entire section with improvements.

Things could not be going better, *so why didn't he feel better about them?* Perhaps he was coming down with something, possibly a cold. He shivered as he looked about and to his surprise he was on Grafton's main street heading not for the hotel but for the marshal's office. The wind whipped his open clawhammer coat and he braced forward into it.

His feet led him not only to the door of the marshal's office but beyond it. He well knew what he was supposed to do. He had assured Isom Rastrow that he would make sure Roy Maginnis, or whoever was on duty at the calaboose, would be safely out of the way when he came to pick up Lefty Price. He had promised to do the same with Doc Whitelaws but it had proven unnecessary. According to Kerry Lu Massingale, the medico had been summoned out to a ranch to attend some bronc buster who had had his leg broken. A bouncer from Hal Owen's Gold Bar Saloon had been posted outside the hospital door to see that the prisoner didn't escape.

Rogan hadn't figured on that, but what could one bouncer do when he came up against Isom Rastrow and his armed men? It didn't occur to the banker that his own wife might have sent the man out to fetch some supper for the prisoner and for Kerry Lu. And even if it had, in his present mood Rogan would not have cared. His despondency had reached such a depth that it was difficult for him to concern himself with anything. He felt somehow that he should go back to the darkened bank and go over his ledger books. Instead he turned into Rawina Pine's trading post.

Susan looking cheerful in a gingham dress and a sweater was putting out the light in the little post office cage when he entered.

"I'm sorry, Mr. Rogan, but we're just closing up for the night."

"That's all right," he said casually. "I sent your mother home with a stew she had spent the better part of the afternoon preparing. I

221

was wondering. . . ."

"Yes, Mr. Rogan . . . ?"

"I was wondering if maybe you and Mrs. Pine would join me in going over to your place and having dinner together."

The words coming out that way astonished Rogan. He had never proposed such a thing in his life. But he had done it tonight.

"Horace!" Rawina Pine said, entering from the storeroom in back. "You're out without a hat. And a man needs a hat in this weather, and a warm coat."

"I . . . I seem to have mislaid my hat, Rawina. Gettin' old, I guess."

"You're no older than I am. Come now. Susan, light the lamps again. We have to find a suitable hat for Horace."

"Did you hear?" Susan asked. "Mr. Rogan wanted to know if we would both join him for dinner at Mom's."

"Small wonder," Rawina Pine said. "It takes a long time to get over the shock of losing a son. I'm not over Noah's death. In fact, I don't know if I ever will be. Rather than getting better, every day that passes it seems worse."

"Do you think that's it?" Rogan asked.

"I wouldn't be at all surprised. Now, Horace, just come over here. I'm sure we have just the thing for you."

222

Rogan absently followed Rawina Pine toward the shelves of head gear in a corner of the back wall.

The women did their level best to ease his mood as he tried on various hats. When he had selected a black John B. with a rounded crown and a modified brim, he gladly paid the fifteen dollars and waited for the women while they finished putting out the lamps and closed up for the night.

The walk to the Gates's place took the banker again past the marshal's office, but this time on the opposite side of the street. Rogan walked on the outside, Rawina in the middle. They told him about Isom Rastrow's visit and how generous he had been in going up into the Neversummers to bring Silas Pine's body back to town for a proper burial. Rogan listened distractedly, still unable to shake loose whatever black emotion had him in its grip.

No one was more surprised, nor in the end more pleased, to see him again that night than Helen Gates. She had suspected how little the man had been enjoying the silent meals with Sarah, when she deigned to dine with him. It appeared the most natural thing in the world that he would be lonely in such a big house.

With three women doing their best to make him comfortable, and finding himself feeling in better spirits when the talk turned to Baby Hope, Rogan was almost looking forward to the stew, bread fresh from the bakery, and the coffee, sitting at the Gates's kitchen table with Rawina while Susan helped her mother. But he never got the chance to sample it.

Hal Owen, his very round face shadowed and fringe of hair concealed by the derby he wore, came to the door. Rogan had been seen heading this way with Rawina and Susan Gates. What Owen had to report wasn't pleasant. Lefty Price had broken jail. Roy Maginnis had been tied up and gagged and left in the cell Price had occupied. Ben Massingale was also gone, and with him his daughter, Kerry Lu, and quite possibly Rogan's wife, Sarah. Judge Tabor was summoning a posse to take out after Isom Rastrow and the others whom Roy had identified. Hal was certain Rogan would want to ride with them. The banker, lulled by the warmth and the talk, was jolted into action and rushed to join the posse. He could hear Rawina's voice calling after them, wanting to know from Hal Owen if this meant that no one would be bringing back Silas Pine's body.

"Women!" Owen remarked in disgust, pulling down his brocaded vest and spitting into the street away from the wind.

Rogan had no answer to that as he hurried

silently beside the saloonkeeper toward Judge Tabor's house. He had no idea how a posse would be able to function any more effectively this night in the dark than had been the case when the bank had been robbed. Despite his accelerated gait, his mind was roaming wildly over the possibilities.

So Sarah had been taken. He had suspected as much. Probably that explained why he had been at such a loss at what to do once he had learned from Mrs. Gates that Sarah had gone to Doc Whitelaws's house.

"They left Maginnis alive, eh?" he gasped to Owen as they hit a stretch of boardwalk.

"Almost didn't," Owen replied. "According to Maginnis, that fellow Price insisted they let him be, that there had been enough killing. If it had been up to Reno Poteet, they would have finished Roy Maginnis fer sure."

Judge Tabor's house was located two city lots down the street from his livery stable and feed barn. Rogan saw horses stamping nervously in the flickering light emitted by hand-held torches wielded by the few men who were mounted. In the illumination shed by the torches the banker could also see Santiago Cruz holding by a leash the bloodhound he used when he went hunting.

"I guess they're going to use the dog to pick up their tracks," Owen said as they came upon the cluster of men in front of the judge's house.

The horses seemed more and more nervous as the mounted men held the torches as high above their heads as they could. The judge was outside, Malinda Tabor at his side. Roy Maginnis was one of the few mounted men without a torch.

"Santiago says Angel can show us the way, men," Maginnis was saying, holding his horse by a tight rein. "The torches should help us. Santiago is going to lead the way. All those who want to join up, get your horses and be back here in five minutes."

"That means us," Hal Owen said to Horace Rogan. "Where's your nag?"

"Back in my stable."

"Well," said the saloonman, "better get a move on if you want to be in on this."

"Since I ain't official in this here job, the jedge is gonna swear you boys in," Maginnis said in his loud, booming voice.

"How can we hold these damned stupid critters down long enough, that's what I wanna know?" one of the mounted men holding a torch bellowed at the blacksmith.

"Gentlemen, please, a little order," Judge Tabor said.

Rogan didn't hear any more as he turned the corner heading up the side street toward his home. Despite the chill wind which had not abated, his face was wreathed with perspiration. He wasn't at all certain where this would lead. His depression was gone, as was his sorrow at parting from Baby Hope. Now the only emotion he seemed to feel was terror and it caused him to quicken his step along the dark street where lights from windows were barely enough to illumine his way.

Chapter Twenty-Three

It was quiet in the darkness of the stable. Isom Rastrow had rolled a cigarette and, taking a match from the block he kept in his shirt pocket, he struck it against the wooden side of a stall. His horse snorted and stamped a foot. He reached over and patted the animal's withers in a reassuring way.

The cold wind had died down somewhat, but drafts of it could still be felt through chinks in the weathered clapboards of the stable. He would have looked at his pocket watch when he had lit the match except that the time didn't really matter. He was certain of his quarry.

Hurried footfalls on the gravel and dirt outside the stable door broke in upon his inner reflections. He took a deep drag on his quirly before dropping it to the hard-packed ground of the stable floor and grinding it out beneath a boot.

There was no moon and little starshine as one of the two stable doors was thrust open, but in the vague lamplight from a back window of the house Rastrow could make out the silhouette of Horace Rogan.

The banker moved cautiously in the dark, feeling his way toward the first stall where he kept his riding horse, a dun gelding.

"Need some light, Rogan?" Rastrow's voice slashed out of the darkness. Then he struck another match. In its flickering gleam, Rogan, who had gasped at the sound of the voice and had drawn back, saw that Rastrow had drawn his gun. It must have been for this purpose that he had struck the match. The wind, blowing in now from the open door, soon extinguished the flame.

"Isom?" Rogan said. "What are you doing here? Don't you know the whole town is hunting for you and your men?"

"Sure do, Horace. And I opine you were about to join in on the hunt."

"Just for the sake of appearances." Rogan's voice sought to convey a casualness he certainly did not feel.

"I won't be keeping you long, Horace." The voice seemed to smile in the darkness. "You know we've got Sarah and Kerry Lu as well as Massingale."

"So I've heard. That wasn't part of the plan."

"It wasn't part of *your* plan. Things are changed from what they were this afternoon. The way I figure it now, the boys an' me are outlawed. But we're not leavin' here with any couple of thousand. The way I got it figgered, the most we get is ten thousand. That's if Massingale tells us where he hid the loot. When he sees what'll happen to Kerry Lu if he don't talk, I reckon he will."

"But . . . ," Rogan interrupted.

"Let me finish, Horace." Rastrow paused, and then he continued. "If, as I'm beginnin' to think, Massingale and his bunch got no loot worth havin', that leaves the boys an' me holdin' an empty bag. Now that's where your wife comes in. There's a price on her head and I 'spect you'll pay it."

"How much?" Rogan's voice, already shaken by his fear and his recent exertion, had become even more choked.

"Ten thousand dollars, Horace. You see? One way or t'other we get ten thousand. If Massingale's got that much hid, we get twice that."

"You must be mad. They're getting a posse comitatus together right now. And they've got a bloodhound."

"Let 'em. Won't do 'em any good on a night like this. An' by tomorrow mornin' I expect you to lead 'em in the wrong direction."

"But I'm not Acting Marshal. I may not even be in time to ride out with the posse."

"Your horse is rested. I figger you'll catch

230

up. Want to know where you'll find your wife?"

"Where?"

"Black Ellis'll be holdin' her at Jake Milton's old place. That's the farthest one of those quarter sections. You got until two nights from now before dusk to get there with the ten thousand. And no funny money. Remember, we don't have to kill Massingale. He could be left to recover and come back. Reckon yuh wouldn't like that much, since yer payin' us to lose him forever."

"You're not giving me enough time, Isom," the banker pleaded.

"I'm givin' yuh all we got. You ever been out to the Milton place?"

"Once. Some time ago."

"Well, mebbe you'll recall that his cabin is built on high ground with a view of the whole valley where those other quarter sections are located. Behind it is a steep outcropping of the Neversummers. Black'll see if'n you bring the posse and he'll plug the old woman if you do. A fast horse out back and he'll be gone before anyone gets to the cabin. If you come alone an' bring the money, you'll have her back."

"How can I do it? Leave with the posse tonight, or catch up with them, and be at the Milton place two nights from tonight before dusk?"

231

"Cain't say as to that. Them's the terms. I just want 'em clear."

"This is murder!"

"Call it what you want." Rastrow's voice, which he had been keeping low and ominous, now lashed out anew at the banker. "You've had it yer own way too long in this game. I've called a new deal. Them's yer cards. Play 'em any way you want. If that posse gets close, we leave 'em Massingale. The girl has been promised to Reno no matter what. Black'll have your old woman at the Milton place. If thet posse follows, she gets a bullet."

Rastrow stirred, moving closer to his horse. He holstered his .45, found the stirrup and mounted. Rogan remained motionless, breathing heavily.

"Figger yuh know what's gotta be done. I done you the service of saddlin' yer bronc fer yuh. Get that posse off our trail and get that money up to the Milton place by dusk two nights from now."

"Wait, Isom. Please wait! How do I know you'll do as you say? What assurance have I, if I do take money from the depositors to pay your ransom, that I'll get Sarah back alive?" He was trembling so as he spoke that it could be heard in his tone.

Isom Rastrow sat atop his horse, silent for a moment in the darkness. He could barely make out the darker shadow of the banker's bulk in the blackness of the stable. It was the last card he had thought of playing in this very close game. He nudged his horse with his knees and presently loomed right beside Horace Rogan. He reached out in the cold drafts of the darkness and grasped the banker by a lapel, pulling him over toward his left stirrup. He was bent down low when he said it.

"How d'yuh know I'm a man of my word, Horace?" he murmured. "I'll tell yuh how. 'Cause it was me what shot Obadiah Rogan that morning, and not Massingale, just as it was me what plugged that boy marshal yuh had."

Rogan let out a sound that might have been a whimper.

"I mean ta get what I want an' I want that money, Rogan. I'd just as soon kill yuh as spit at yuh. But I'm givin' you a chance to save yer wife. It don't get no plainer than thet."

With this last word, he thrust out with his arm and sent the banker reeling backwards to collapse in a heap in front of the forward stall.

"Remember. Two nights from now. Before dusk."

Rastrow's horse moved then, bulking in the

dim light emanating from the rear window of the house, and passed out into the night. He obviously was circling around behind the stable and heading out of town that way.

Horace Rogan slowly and painfully rose to his knees and then to his feet. He paused in the darkness to brush off his pants' legs. And then, his face awash with sweat, his body trembling uncontrollably, he groped his way to the side of the forward stall and vomited.

Chapter Twenty-Four

Silas Pine's fever broke shortly before dawn.
It was then that he began trembling from the
cold. Even with the fire's blaze, which Shawn
stoked with what remained of the dry wood,
and with every available blanket covering him,
there seemed to be no way to control the ef-
fects of the internal chill and the gusty drafts
which swept in through the mouth of the cave.
To minimize the impact of the smoke from
the fire, Shawn had had to position it closer
to the opening of the cave than toward the
rear.

There had been little sleep for her that night
since Shawn had awakened the first time. Now
with Pine's body being wracked by involuntary spasms of shivering, Shawn moved herself
closer to him, trying to turn him on his right
side enough for her to put her right arm over
him and hold the coverings securely.

Pulling one blanket up so it covered their
heads slightly, she felt that perhaps the
warmth of her breath between their bodies
would help. For a while the trembling actually
subsided. Then, with a mutter and stirring,

Pine leaned too far over, slipping from her grasp. He came to rest on his bandaged and exposed back and a grunt of pain escaped his lips. Shawn rose to her knees, still under the covers, intent on turning Pine's body back so it was resting again on his right side.

His was a dead weight. She didn't want to wrench him too abruptly, but now his body began arching upward, raising his lacerated back off the ground cover. He groaned mournfully. Shawn threw back the cover, determined to free herself sufficiently from the enveloping covers to move him.

Dawn in the higher reaches, when the skies are not overcast, happens suddenly. It was like that now, with a bright, languid glow penetrating through the cave's maw. Pine groaned again, resisting Shawn's struggles, and then she saw that his eyes were open.

"Miz . . . Miz Massingale . . . ?" he gasped, seemingly remembering nothing from the previous evening.

Shawn looked from his grizzled face to the light outside the cave and back again.

"The day's come unco' soon," she said. "For your own sake, Silas, will ye na fight me more and roll onto your stomach, or I'll no bear the wyte of it if you begin bleeding again."

Pine only nodded his head slowly. He

grunted with the effort and seemed unable to raise himself, although not for want of trying. Shawn kept tugging at his right shoulder and hip and, with another groan of pain, succeeded in turning the man onto his belly.

"Ay, now, that's better," Shawn said, breathing out a sigh.

She extricated herself completely from the blankets and wrapped them around Pine's prostrate body as best she could.

"Miz . . . ," Silas began, his voice very hoarse, then he corrected himself, as if some faint recollection had come back to him of their time at the mountain stream. "Shawn," he whispered, "is there any water?"

"If ye'll promise to lie there still and make nae a move, I shall go and fill the canteen. Ye'll have water and, if ye are able, a dram of brandy as well from the little flask I brought."

Silas's face, still contorted by ripples of pain, brightened and he nodded. He watched her silently, as she stood up, grasped the sheepskin coat around her, bent over to pick up the canteen which rested near the fire, and made her way slowly toward the mouth of the cave. The dawn light, reflecting on the thin patina of snow from the previous night, glistened so that it hurt Shawn's eyes as she emerged from the semi-darkness within.

Presently she returned. Pine in the meantime had managed to get his elbows beneath his body so that he could more easily hold up his head. To move still caused him grief, but at least it was tolerable.

Shawn poured a little of the icy cold water into a metal cup and held it to Pine's lips. He drank rapidly at first, until she pulled the cup away. Pine's right arm jerked free so he might grab at the cup, but a sharp jab of pain stopped him short.

"Slowly, now, Silas," Shawn warned.

"God, it's cold," he said. Then he leaned forward to drink again from the cup which once more she held close to his lips.

When he had almost consumed the entire cup with small gulps, pausing for breath as she pulled it away for a moment and then returned it, she filled it partially with more water from the canteen and added to this a spot of brandy from the small bottle she had brought with the medical supplies.

That first drink had made Silas think that his teeth would crack from the coldness of it, but this was now offset by the warmth the brandy seemed to spread throughout him inside. He even felt vigorous enough after the first swallow to prop himself up high using his elbows and the pain, while present, did not overwhelm him the way it had the evening before when, he now remembered, he had tried to crawl after Shawn in the snow.

"I'll change your dressings after I've cut some bacon and get it to frying," she told him, once the brandy and water were gone.

Letting himself gently down onto his upper body, Pine watched Shawn as she went about banking the fire and slicing bacon from a slab she had in a burlap sack along with the bread she had brought.

"Na doubt, ye couldna eat night last, Silas," she said. "How's the appetite this morn?"

"Last night's still a little vague, Shawn," he said as she worked. "But it's coming back in bits and pieces. I can tell you this. I'm famished . . . and thirsty."

"Ay, a good sign," she said.

"The bear, that crazy she-bear?" he asked.

"Dead."

"You?"

"Na, na, it was Ben. And when she hit him, it was that man who replaced your son as marshal who finished her, him and that deputy ye sent packing that time back at our place."

"Rastrow and Poteet." It was a statement.

"Ay. They left ye behind but took my Ben with them."

"Do you think Ben's all right?"

"I ken that not, Silas. I skulked about to see after ye once they left. If I'd found ye dead, I would have followed."

"Sorry you had to stay behind."

"I'm not," she said firmly, fixing her eyes on him, her manner solemn. "Alone there's little I could have done for my Ben." She paused for only an instant before dropping her eyes back to the last slice of bacon she arranged in the small fry pan. "You still think Ben killed Noah."

"Not likely," Silas said stiffly. "Before that bear hit us he even satisfied me that he hadn't any of the loot from that bank robbery."

There were now tears glistening in Shawn's eyes but she said nothing.

"I reckon I almost did a terrible wrong to you . . . and to your husband." Pine stirred beneath his covers, grimaced, and then did his best to smile at her. "I'm not in very good shape. I don't know what can be done with me."

"That occurred to me night last," Shawn said, as she placed the fry pan on the hot coals of the fire. "Adakhai's village is closest. If there's need for a doctor, maybe Gage Cameron could ride to town for Doc Whitelaws."

"Not if you can get me to Adakhai's people," Pine said, the trace of a smile returning to his lips. "I was once married to a Navajo woman. They've got a concoction she once used on me when I got hit by a trap-jumper's bullet. I know there's powdered cedar-pine needles in it and rattlesnake oil and what not. But it did the job."

"All I have is carbolic acid," Shawn said, and turned bacon with the tip of a hunting knife.

Although it was moderately awkward, Pine was able to put away his share of bacon and bread, washed down with water, provided Shawn fed him by hand and held the cup for him. She had put on coffee while they were eating and it was ready once they'd finished. Shawn laced a little of the brandy into the coffee for Pine.

"This Navajo woman ye married," she said, drawing the tin coffee cup away from Silas as he swallowed, "was she the reason ye left Rawina?"

"No," Pine said slowly. "That was later, after Rawina had already left with . . . with our son. It jest got too lonely for her, being a trapper's wife, with me gone so much of the time. She wanted the boy — Noah — to have a proper education and things like that and I jest couldn't bring myself to livin' in any town or being a farmer or working on a ranch. I'd tried those things and it was no good. I had got used to being by myself and didn't care a whole lot for having a lot of people around. It was all right to go among 'em

241

for supplies and maybe a drink or two once in a while. But, otherwise, I was happiest by myself. It weren't Rawina's fault. Mine, if anyone's to blame. We jest wanted different things out of life."

Shawn held the cup of steaming coffee again to his lips. The brandy had cooled it sufficiently that he could take a bigger gulp than at first.

"One winter after Rawina and Noah had left, it was bitterly cold with one blizzard after another. I had visited Adakhai's camp a few times and spent a week there once trading with his people. When a break came in the weather, I set out for it and was able to get there before the next blizzard broke. Cost me my horse, but I made it. It was that winter I met Sah-Nee. Or, I should say, Adakhai chose her for me. Her parents were both dead and she had no family left. She was what you would call his ward, I guess. The price was ten horses. But because it was a bad winter, come spring we settled for twenty double eagles, jest about all I had been able to save in the four years of trapping once Rawina left."

"Were ye both happy together?"

Silas Pine was quiet for a time. "Women are tough as hell," he said then. "They really are. White men try puttin' 'em on a pedestal, try to coddle 'em, protect 'em. But we suffer more in the end than they do. Never sell 'em short. Out here a woman takes her place alongside a man. They build together, suffer together. And they'll fight for a cause, jest like you're doin' for your family."

"Was Sah-Nee tough?" Shawn asked, sipping her own coffee, her knees drawn up tightly, sitting near where Pine reclined.

"Not as tough as Rawina, I reckon. Look what Rawina's done. She's got her own business, made it on her own, entire. Sah-Nee was just as tough, maybe, but in her own way, and not so tough at all when it came to white man's disease. That's what I believe to this day killed her. I went in among them and I came back and she fell ill. It was probably something I brought back with me. It hit her and not me. Indians are like that. They don't have our centuries of drunkenness, so it don't take much at all to get 'em drunk. The same with our diseases. We can fight 'em off easier because we been doin' it longer."

"What did you do once she died?"

"Trapped for a while and then started comin' back to see Noah. It never worked out, but I kept trying. Until two years ago, when I gave up for good."

"Ye couldn'a given up, Silas, or ye wouldn'a be here now?"

"I had, though. It wasn't until I went to

an army doctor about being short of breath sometimes and feeling sick to my stomach. I thought it was some sickness I had. He told me it was my heart. That it was giving out. He couldn't even tell me how long I had. Jest be grateful for every day, he said, and rest and avoid strain."

Shawn's brow had been furrowed until she heard this last comment. She could not prevent the grin that lighted her features.

"Ye're still here, Silas," she said, "and after what a strain!"

Pine could not help smiling himself, even if a bit wistfully. "I reckon I got no business being alive after all the punishment I've given myself since the day I got into town. Yet, here I am. You're right, Shawn. By rights, I should've been dead when that bear hit me, not from the bear, but from my heart. I even thought about that while it was happening." He stopped, as if lost suddenly in thought. "No, you're right, Shawn, I got no business being alive, but. . . ."

"Here," she said, picking up his coffee cup and holding it for him, "finish this. Then I'll look to changing your dressings and feeding my horse. I also have to find more firewood."

"What about them wolves?" Silas asked, as he swallowed the last of it.

"Didna see naething of them when I went for water."

"That don't mean they're not around. But, as a rule, they don't tend to bother humans."

"And don't forget that she-bear."

"No," Silas admitted, "that should have been enough to hold a sizable pack of 'em for a spell."

Shawn tended to Pine's wounds and gave him more water to drink. She gave the roan half the oats she had brought and led her outside later to drink. Chooky had already relieved herself in the cave twice and Shawn did her best to clean it up and with pine branches sweep that portion of the rock floor. She went over her food supplies and, if rationed properly, the two of them might make it another three days, the roan two before the oats were gone entirely.

Pine was sleeping for most of this time. Because of its thickness, Shawn had her prized Navajo rug between him and the floor and all the covers packed around him. Getting firewood had been a challenge, but the weather helped some. Snow was still on the ground, but it was slushy and the wind that blew softly through the lodgepoles and stunted pine was damp, penetrating but not frigid. There was a deadfall near the stream, rotten on the side, and relatively dry, which furnished her with enough wood for six trips to the cave. She relieved herself twice in the course of the day on the side of the outcropping in which the cave was located and knew that the most difficult journey was yet ahead of her that day when she must see that Pine was able to do so.

The roan was back inside the cave and safely tethered when Shawn went out to refill the canteen at the stream. The light was beginning rapidly to fade as dusk softly engulfed the rugged terrain. She was entering the cave for what she supposed would be the final time after doing chores. Now would come the ordeal of waking Pine and moving him either far back into the cave or just outside of it so he could relieve himself when she caught sight of movement from the corner of her eyes.

She ducked into the cave's maw and then, cautiously, looked out down the trail up which she had ridden and Rastrow and Poteet had disappeared with Ben. It was a lone rider on a black horse. He would surely have seen her but he was keeping his eyes to the ground, as if trailing someone and looking for tracks.

"Shawn!" she heard Pine's voice rasp from inside the cave. He must have just awakened. "What is it? Is it someone coming?"

"Hush," she said, drawing back. "I ken not for certain, but it might be one of those lying sneck-draws that works as a deputy. Now, hush, I say."

Removing her high-crowned hat, Shawn peered once more around the corner of the cave. The man had dismounted and was pawing around the ground beneath a tree with the toe of one boot. Then he stooped down and brushed away snow heavy with moisture with his gloved hands. It wasn't until he began examining some flat, silvery objects he had picked up from the ground, and had turned his head as best he could to take advantage of the failing light, that Shawn moved.

Pine, having swiveled himself around slowly and painfully so he could watch, saw the woman reach under her sheepskin coat, draw out a pistol, and step outside the cave. He tried to pull himself forward with his arms braced under him, but the instant shock of pain from the region of his back stopped him. He could do nothing but lie there, and listen, and wait.

Chapter Twenty-Five

It was still dark when the wagon and the riders pulled into the ranch yard outside Jake Milton's place. Of the four homesteads Isom Rastrow had once hoped to weld together into a horse ranch, this one had the finest cabin and outbuildings, including a sturdy two-story barn and a squat bunkhouse. Milton, when he had first settled here, had had more money than the others and had even been able to hire men to help him around the place. Two bad winters in a row and a summer drought, however, had been more than he was able to sustain and so he had been forced to mortgage the place to the bank. Once he had become in default of his payments, Rogan had warned him that foreclosure was imminent.

Now Jake Milton was dead and it was anyone's guess what would happen to his place. Rastrow, when his plan for the horse ranch seemed possible, had opined that he would make this his headquarters. He had had to forego his dream, but he didn't intend to leave the region with empty pockets.

"Easy inside there," he said, guiding his

horse alongside the wagon through the snow which had begun to fall and reining up near the tailgate. "Black, you go inside the cabin and strike lights. Bring back a lantern. Reno, you and Lefty stay out here with me. No one gets out until Black comes back."

Presently a light appeared through the front window and then another one obviously farther back, in the smaller adjacent room, appeared throwing a yellow illumination off to the side. The sky was overcast and so starshine was of no help. There was no moon. The large snowflakes dimmed visibility even more.

"Reckon we've got a blizzard on our hands?" Poteet asked, edging his horse close to where Rastrow sat his gelding.

"Naw, not cold enough," Rastrow said. "I figure this'll turn to rain before long. Lucky for us, though. It'll make trackin' us all the harder for any posse they got roamin' about, although I told Rogan it was up to him to see they didn't find us."

"You sure he can be trusted?" Poteet asked. "Seems to me he's double-crossed us more'n once."

"In this here case, I do. If'n he wants to see his missus again, he's got to play along. Besides, I told him that it was me that plugged his kid, not Massingale. That's gonna show him we mean business if anything will."

Poteet glanced anxiously toward the tarpaulin covering the wagon bed, knowing Rogan's wife was in there and wondering if she had heard. Something had changed in Isom Rastrow. He'd become reckless. To Poteet, this whole play seemed more dangerous than it was worth.

"It took you long enough," Rastrow said gruffly as Black Ellis moved closer to them, holding an Argand lamp in front of him.

"I couldn't find this one right away," Ellis said. He was shielding the glass spout as best he could from the snow.

"All right," Rastrow said. "Lefty, you and Reno start undoing those cords."

Price had climbed down from the front seat while they had been waiting for Ellis to return. Now, Poteet dismounted and the two of them began untying the tail end of the tarpaulin. Rastrow had drawn his six-gun, a double-cocker, and drew back the hammer twice while Ellis crowded in closer to the rear, holding the lamp above the wagon bed.

"I figure we should leave the front tied down," Poteet said when they had loosened the lashings just beyond midway.

"Okay, all you inside," Rastrow said in a loud voice. "We're going to pull back the tarpaulin. Don't nobody try to make a run for it, or you're dead."

Poteet on the left side and Price on the right began to pull the tarpaulin back slowly. Sarah Rogan was slumped in the rear and was the first to sit up, her dark eyes blinking in the flickering light of the elevated lamp. Massingale was lying cross-wise with Kerry Lu cuddled beside him.

"Get that light over there, closer to Massingale," Rastrow said. Ellis moved the lamp alongside Massingale. "What do you know? The bad man is awake?"

Kerry Lu struggled up to her knees. "What do you intend doing to my Dad? Why have you brought us here?"

"If I were you, Missy, I'd worry more about what Reno and the boys here will be doin' to you if we don't find that money your father hid."

"There is no money," Massingale managed to gasp.

"Enough palaverin'," Rastrow ordered. "Black, you keep that light where we can see everyone. You women climb down outa there. Reno, you and Lefty get up there and give Massingale a hand. Looks like he'll be needin' one."

The snow was indeed turning to a light rain as Sarah Rogan, followed by Kerry Lu, and then Massingale supported on either side by Poteet and Lefty followed Black Ellis up the three steps to the small roofed porch and inside the cabin. Rastrow had tied his horse to a wagon wheel and followed behind, still holding his gun at the ready.

Once inside, Sarah Rogan and Kerry Lu were told to sit on the floor in the far left corner. A table and three straight-back chairs were in the center of the room and Massingale was eased into one of the chairs.

"Black, get a fire goin' in that stove. Lefty, look to the horses and get that wagon under cover in the barn. Reno, you watch the old woman and the girl. Massingale and I have to settle somethin'."

Reno Poteet leered at Kerry Lu as he stood over her. Sarah Rogan seemed not to notice him. She was staring fixedly at Isom Rastrow who placed a booted foot on one of the chairs and rested the cocked six-gun on his knee.

Massingale was extremely pale and seemed to have trouble breathing. "Why'd you bring those two along?" he whispered hoarsely, his words broken.

"Why'n't you make this easy on everybody, Massingale?" Rastrow said. "You didn't have the money on you when we come on you up on the mountain side. That means you must of hid it. We want it. If you tell us where it's at, you and your young'un over there get to go just as soon as we settle with Rogan.

If you don't, you get to see the boys have a little fun with Kerry Lu. I figger you're tough. Tougher'n the rest of that riffraff that pulled the job. That's why you're alive and they ain't. But you ain't so tough that you're likely to put that money which you'll never see nohow above seein' the pain the boys'll cause Kerry Lu."

"You . . . do . . . anything to hurt . . . Kerry Lu and I swear. . . ."

"Save it," Rastrow broke in. "You ain't in no position to do nothing to nobody. You got one choice and that's to sing out."

Poteet had turned slightly to watch this interchange. Ellis was still getting a blaze going in the firebox of the stove. Kerry Lu had one hand in her mouth and her eyes, too, were on her father and Rastrow.

It was then that Sarah Rogan made her move. Poteet wasn't aware of it until he felt the tug of his six-gun as it left the leather of his holster. He slapped downward with his hand and pivoted.

Sarah Rogan had backed up swiftly, cocking the six-gun as she moved, holding it with both hands and aiming it toward Isom Rastrow.

"You crazy, lady?" Rastrow asked, his face flushing with anger. "Give that gun back to Reno and no one'll get hurt."

"I'll give you what's in it," she rasped, the

sights now level with Rastrow's chest.

"She heard what you said about her son," Poteet said. "Out there at the wagon. She didn't know you was only jokin', Isom."

"Ben Massingale!" Sarah Rogan's voice lashed across the room. "Who killed Obbie?"

"I don't rightly . . . know . . . Miz Rogan," he said slowly, his head lolling toward her. "None of us . . . did . . . for him. We were . . . his partners. We were . . . supposed to meet . . . here at Jake's . . . after. . . ."

"Lady," Rastrow commanded, "I told you to put up that gun less'n you want to get killed." His own six-gun was still in his hand and still cocked, but he made no overt move.

Black Ellis had a blaze going in the stove but he, too, remained squatting. He didn't figure he had the time to draw and fire before the mad woman could fire a shot at Rastrow.

The very moment Rastrow saw the twitch in her eyes, he lunged sideways, bringing his six-gun around and firing point blank as he fell. The two shots were very nearly simultaneous. Sarah Rogan's spatted into the wall behind where Rastrow had been standing. Rastrow's slug, fired as he was moving, struck the small woman through the neck, slamming her back against the wall, the gun clattering to the floor. She made a choking sound and then collapsed.

Even as she was still falling, Massingale was out of his chair. It must have been his intention to grab at Rastrow's gun. But he was too slow. Rastrow, now on his side on the floor, rolled over and again cocked his six-gun.

"Try it, and you're dead."

Massingale halted, freezing, and then began wobbling. Poteet rushed up and grabbed hold of him. Turning Massingale around toward him, he sent a fist into his face, knocking the wounded man backwards toward the table. He fell on top of it and it tipped over. Massingale landed on the other side.

Black Ellis had now drawn his six-gun also. He rose and covered Massingale. The outlaw did not move.

Lefty Price, who had heard the shots out in the barn, now barged in the front door, his own six-gun drawn.

"What happened?" he said.

"I had to plug the old woman," Rastrow said, rising to his feet. "She pulled Reno's gun when he wasn't looking and tried to kill me."

"You killed a woman?" Lefty was staring with disbelief at the blood that had flowed blackly from Sarah Rogan's throat onto the floor.

"Seems like we broke you outa jail for doin' the same," Poteet said.

255

"She maybe died when I was with her," Lefty said, angrily holstering his six-gun, "but it was your gun barrel that did it."

Kerry Lu had scampered across the room to kneel beside her father. Black now raised his gun to cover her.

"What the hell's happenin' to this outfit?" Price demanded, his voice high-pitched. "I thought we was goin' to settle down to horseranchin'. Instead, it's been nothin' but killin' an' more killin'. Rogan's kid, that tin-star, Crowley's woman, old man Pine, and now the old woman! Where's it gonna stop? They'll hang us, sure!"

"Easy," Rastrow said. He turned his gun calmly on Lefty Price. "You sayin' you want out?"

Price blinked but did not answer.

"Well?" Rastrow asked.

"I just want the killing to stop, Isom." His voice now held a note of defeat.

"It's stopped, Lefty," Rastrow assured him. "All we got left to do is find out where Massingale over there hid the loot and collect from Rogan, and then we're all hittin' leather."

"There's a bed in back, boss," Black Ellis said. "You want we should move Massingale back there?"

Rastrow was still confronting Lefty Price and seemed not to have heard. Poteet walked over toward Sarah Rogan's body, stooped, and picked up his gun. He ejected the spent casing and drew another brass-capped slug from his gunbelt.

"What about Massingale, boss?" Black Ellis repeated.

"Aw, go on and finish up with the horses," Rastrow said to Lefty Price, the corners of his mouth grimacing in a tight smile.

"Keno," Price said, and walked back out the front door, closing it behind him.

"No, I don't want Massingale moved," Rastrow said, turning to Ellis. "You an' Reno heft the old lady into the other room. She'll make a nice little package for that double-crossin' son-of-a-bitch when he gets here with the money." He laughed gruffly.

"Daddy," Kerry Lu whispered. She was caressing his head and sobbing silently, the tears dropping out of her eyes onto her father's face.

Ellis and Poteet hefted the old woman between them and carried her out of the room. Isom Rastrow crept down beside Kerry Lu. He had holstered his six-gun.

"He'll be all right, Missy," he said. "Your Daddy will need a lot more than that to kill him."

"Why don't you do something for him, then?" Kerry Lu demanded, snuffling and brushing the tears from her eyes with a sleeve of her dress.

"Tell you what I'll do," Rastrow said quietly. "I'll get somethin' for you to put behind his head." He rose again to his feet. "Then we'll try to bring him around. What do you say to that?"

"Just stop hurting him," she sobbed aloud. "Just stop hurting everyone."

Rastrow was sufficiently confident that Kerry Lu wouldn't make a break for the door. He followed Ellis and Poteet into the back room where Jake Milton had slept to fetch back a pillow.

Chapter Twenty-Six

Lefty Price was able to see only vaguely. The sun had crept behind the highest peaks of the Neversummers and lit the approaching figure from behind, a crimson aureole surrounding the silhouette as it advanced. The peaked hat shadowed the face. Lefty could see that the figure was holding a six-gun.

"Have ye found my Ben's money, what he stole from the bank?" Shawn asked tartly.

"Miz Massingale?" Price's face, accentuated in the reddish light, reflected his astonishment even more than did his voice.

"Ay, and who maught ye be?"

"Lefty Price, ma'am. I was one of them with Isom Rastrow, but I quit him. I was on my way, headin' outa these parts, and I jest thought I'd have a look-see if Ben had told the truth."

Shawn paused about six feet from the squat, compact man.

"And where were ye to hear truth from Ben's lips."

"It was in the Grafton jail, ma'am. I was bein' held there, but that's another story. I

259

was there when they brung your man in. He had passed out on the way into town and they left him in the cell next to mine and sent for the doc. Your daughter, Kerry Lu, she was there, and after a spell Ben come around. He was full o' questions at first, where he was, what'd happen to old Mr. Pine, the dead marshal's pa, and that sort of thing. Kerry Lu told him Pine was dead, killed in these here mountains. Then Ben remembered the bear, the she-bear that Isom and Reno shot when they came upon 'em. He told her he was showin' Pine these here washers buried right here, near this aspen tree, when that she-bear hit 'em, that there hadn't been no money."

"Ay, that I ken only too well," Shawn said, her voice hard. "Ye must have thought Ben was nae telling the truth." She fell silent and thrust the six-gun toward the man, taking grip of the butt with both hands. "Are ye alone?"

"I done tol' you, ma'am, I quit the bunch. I knew from what Reno'd said that your husband was caught just about where this place was." He paused to doff his hat. His bald head glistened with sweat. He wiped a sleeve across his forehead. "Was I checkin' out what Ben'd said? I reckon you might say so, but I found what I expected. Nothin'."

"Ye just decided of a sudden to quit?"

"Not of a sudden, ma'am. It got so I couldn't take the killin' any more. Too many are daid now, and fer what? Even the money won't mean much when they get it. Not now."

Shawn was puzzled by almost everything this man had said to her. She came rapidly to a decision.

"I donna ken if ye're telling the truth or nae, but the fact is I have need of ye. Back at that cave yonder — the she-bear's own cave, mind ye — is Silas Pine."

"Daid?"

"Na. Very much alive, but badly mauled. I must get him to Adakhai's village a short piece from here, but I na ken how to do it by my lonesome. At least I didna till ye showed up."

"Rastrow and Poteet told everyone in town that old Pine was dead, ma'am. They was even lyin' to his . . . well, that Rawina woman he used to be married to, as how's they was gonna come back and bury him. I had something like that in mind when I headed up here. I ain't proud o' what's been happenin' and I'm glad to be away from it. I woulda done it, though, ma'am. I'm not like the others. That old man has been wronged plenty."

Shawn backed up a pace and turned slightly.

"I want for ye to walk afore me to that cave

261

yonder," she said, still holding the six-gun with two hands. "Walk slowly."

Price put his hat back on and started moving in the direction she indicated. The sun glare, as it set, was harsh on his eyes and he found he had to squint and look down toward his feet as he walked. It was only a slight incline, but the elevation tended to make breathing labored.

Pine, by straining and struggling, had been able to reach the rifle leaning against the cave wall and now held it awkwardly beneath him, supporting himself on his elbows. He knew Lefty Price by sight. As the two forms approached the cave, he peered off into the distance bathed in reds and dark browns in every direction, to see if he could spot anyone else who might have accompanied the captive.

When Price reached the cave's mouth, he stopped and elevated his hands above his head, something he had not done when only Shawn had had him covered. It must have been Pine's eyes, which glared out from under his graying, matted hair with an incredible suppressed fury.

"Just edge along beside me, Price," Pine said, rolling on his side and still holding the rifle. "When you get near the fire, stop."

Price did as he was told, bowing his head slightly although it was unnecessary. When

262

he drew toward the fire, he paused, his hands still elevated.

"Now," Pine said to Shawn who had followed Price into the cave, "lift his six-gun. I'll keep him covered."

"He says he's alone, Silas," Shawn said, holding her own weapon in her right hand and taking Price's with her left.

"It's the truth, ma'am, I swear it," Price said.

"You can sit down," Pine told him, "right after Shawn frisks you for a hide-out. Then you can let your hands down, but keep them where I can see them."

Shawn searched the captive thoroughly and then he sat down, cross-legged, beside the fire.

Pine dragged and pulled himself further around and then edged closer to the fire by using his elbows, keeping the rifle suspended in his hands. Shawn moved over to Price's left, so they had him between a cross-fire should he try to bolt.

"I reckon you know a lot, Lefty," Pine said, once Shawn had settled herself, Price's six-gun by her side, hers still in her right hand.

"Reckon I do, Mr. Pine," Price said. "But like I tol' Miz Massingale here, I've quit the bunch. I was on my way south and stopped here. I had it in mind to bury yuh."

"After ye saw there was nae loot," Shawn reminded him.

"Can't blame a man for seein' for hisself, ma'am. The fact is, right now you need me to help with Mr. Pine here. I'll do it. I'll help you anyway you want and I'll tell yuh what I know, but when we get Mr. Pine where you want him took, I want to be free to travel on. Them's my terms."

Pine bristled at the thought of an outlaw dictating terms. Shawn looked at him dubiously and then back at Price.

"Ye said ye was in jail with Ben. How'd that happen."

"Warn't none of my doin', ma'am. The fiercest black Injun I ever seen found me tendin' to Miz Crowley when she died and she took me in to Grafton and I was put in jail."

"Aurelia's dead?" Shawn asked quietly.

"I had nothin' to do with that," Price said. "I was tol' by Reno to watch her, that's all. He's the one who cracked her on the head with his six-gun. That's what she died from. That crack on her skull." He shook his head and, again, removed his hat. He undid his neckerchief and wiped the sweat from his brow and then mopped his bald head. The narrow tuft of hair was plastered down and glistened in the firelight.

"Do you know who killed my son, Noah?" Pine asked in a guarded voice.

"Reckon I do, Mr. Pine."

Pine nodded in Shawn's direction. "You'd call it dealin' with the divil, Shawn, but I say, we take his offer." Pine's gaze returned to Price. "You unload all you know and you help us get to Adakhai's camp, and you have our word. You'll be free to go from there."

Price was lost in reflection for a few moments. His face showed the play of emotions ranging inside of him. He rubbed his hands nervously along the thighs of his waist overalls.

"I've the makings," Shawn said, reaching into her shirt pocket inside her sheepskin coat which was open. She flipped the sack of tobacco and papers to Price.

"Why, thank you, ma'am."

He laboriously rolled a cigarette. Then, reached out for a small, partially burning stick from the fire, lit it with deliberation.

"Neither of yuh are goin' to like what I tell you one bit," he said, exhaling smoke. "I'm sorry I was ever a part of it. But it's done now, and I cain't go back."

It took more than a half hour for Price to tell them his side of the story, starting with his arrival in Grafton with Isom Rastrow and the others and the deal Horace Rogan had struck with Rastrow once he learned that his son had planned a raid on the bank. At various points in the story, Shawn either nodded or agreed aloud with what he claimed had happened.

Price merely confirmed what had become a growing suspicion about how Noah had met his death. Once he had come to believe Ben Massingale that he hadn't done it, Pine knew it had to have been a posse member. The likely choices had been Isom Rastrow and Reno Poteet. Now there was no question about it.

Once Price got to what had happened that morning at Jake Milton's cabin, Shawn became frantic. She even rose from where she was sitting and looked anxiously out of the cave mouth into the encroaching darkness.

"I'd best be gang, Silas."

"That wouldn't be a good idea, ma'am," Price said, trying to calm her. "They's three armed men at that cabin, even supposin' they're still there. Ben ain't tellin' 'em a thing about where he hid the money."

"But there is nae money!" Shawn said.

"I know it," Price said. "You know it. But Isom and the others don't. That's what's keepin' Ben alive and Kerry Lu from bein' hurt. You couldn't save 'em and likely would make it worse."

"As much as I hate to admit it, Shawn,"

Pine said, "he's right. You'd be better off heading into Grafton and getting together a posse to back your play. But even that is taking a chance. Best would be one or two men going out there unseen until they could work up on the cabin and surprise them." He paused for a moment. "Price can see that I get to Adakhai's camp. You can leave now and probably make town before dawn."

"Ay, and leave ye and this one. Na. I'll see you with Adakhai first."

Her manner was such that Pine argued no further. Shawn did leave the group to fetch Price's gray, which she led over to a grassy patch where the snow had melted near the swift-flowing creek and hobbled him for the night. She thought once or twice that she heard an animal, possibly a wolf, moving in the underbrush, and the mournful wail of a distant coyote broke the night's stillness.

With Price's help, Shawn was able to drag Pine out of the cave in order for him to relieve himself. Pine was grateful when the two walked away a distance so he could have some privacy, but manipulating his fingers to unfasten his pants and keeping himself from touching his back was sufficiently difficult to make him break out in a cold sweat and for a time waves of nausea swept over him. He cursed his weakness.

A meal of sorts was prepared. The bread was stale but the coffee was hot and warming in the dank chill of the cave. They finished the last of the bacon and Shawn fed nearly all of the remaining oats to Chooky.

Pine's dressings were changed again before they bedded down for the night. Shawn could see some improvement. Silas had to admit that the itching was almost as bothersome as the occasional stabs of pain.

Rather than tying Price up for the night, Shawn and Pine took turns keeping watch, relieving each other every two hours. Pine was on watch when the first light of predawn filtered gently across the Neversummers. He roused the others. After another trip for everyone to relieve themselves, they ate what was left of the food and drank the last of the coffee. Shawn gathered sapling boughs and together with Price they followed Pine's directions in fashioning a travois held together with strips of a rawhide riata cut up for the purpose.

Price helped Shawn lift Pine and half carry him over to the travois once it was hitched to Price's gray gelding. Blankets and Shawn's Navajo rug had been placed over the travois and Pine rested on these on his stomach. What of the camp gear could be packed on Chooky's back was taken; the rest left behind.

It was slow going, Shawn taking point, leading Chooky behind her by the reins as she walked. Price led the gelding with Pine dragging along in the rear. They had to keep to the valleys and lower areas, avoiding stands of trees or more treacherous trails along rock outcroppings. In many places the snow had drifted and had not melted, forcing them to seek a way around it and a couple of times, although it was tough-going, across it. Shawn kept looking at the sun and estimating their progress. She figured they'd probably arrive in the late afternoon.

They paused now and then to rest the animals. Walking over this terrain was uncomfortable at best. They paused once to replenish the canteens at a mountain stream. Pine was still consumed with a great thirst.

The warmth of the sun had diminished as it fell in fiery hues behind the peaks of the Neversummers. They crossed a couple of heavily brushed ridges and then saw directly below them a spare layout of hogans. This was the camp of Adakhai and his clan. Spirals of smoke curled up from the fires and bore with them the odors of burnt wood, of the strong smells of sumac and piñon gum, of the greasy taint of mutton being broiled. They made their way slowly and wearily down into the camp.

Shawn had been rather close to the mark in estimating the time it would take them to make this journey afoot. It was dusk. The sun, glinting off the distant snow-capped peaks, seemed to her at once majestic and forbidding and aloof.

Two of Adakhai's young granddaughters greeted them with pleasure when the travois paused near the opening to Adakhai's hogan. Actually, according to Navajo custom, it was the hereditary lodge of the old shaman's last wife. But there was little doubt that Adakhai presided over it and this entire small conclave of Navajos. The stacked-up house was a large hogan made of pine logs, boughs, and cedar and showed some evidence of the white man's road. It boasted somewhat more in room and comfort than the old-style, forked-together hogans whose structure *Hastseyal'ti*, the Talking God, had decreed ages in the past.

Shawn led Chooky to the side of the hogan where she could tie her to a bush. When she came back around front again, one of the granddaughters had just entered the lodge to inform Adakhai of the return of the man who had married Sah-Nee and had lived with them. The other was speaking with Silas Pine as he remained prostrate on the travois. Lefty Price was looking around nervously, not knowing what he might find, but fearful that his presence would be discovered by that black Navajo who had brought him into town from the Crowley place.

When the granddaughter who had entered the lodge peered out again, she made a beckoning sign that they were to enter. Shawn and Price helped Silas Pine to his feet. It struck Shawn at once that pride stiffened Silas, for he held himself as erect as he could and tried to move his legs and feet. They all had to bow down at the low entrance and this caused Silas's feet to drag somewhat behind him.

A trench full of banked coals glowed in the middle of the dirt floor. Adakhai sat cross-legged on a sheepskin pallet at its far side. Pine was lowered gently down on the near side of the fire. He rolled onto his side and supported himself with his right elbow.

"*Xoxo nanaxi, Hatali,*" he said, his voice solemn and respectful. "Long life and happiness, man of medicine."

"*Ahalani, Tsin-tzahn'jih Hatal',*" the shaman said with no less formality, his voice rustling like dry leaves in an autumn breeze. "Greetings, man from the timber."

"*Belinkana* must go," the granddaughter who had led the way now whispered to Shawn, tugging at the sleeve of her sheepskin coat.

Shawn shook her off.

"*Belinkana* must go," the girl repeated, this

271

time more forcefully.

"It is well, Shawn," Silas said, looking now at her, smiling.

Shawn nodded, saying nothing, but there were tears in her eyes. She turned and followed the Navajo girl back through the low entrance. Price was confused. He knew he had kept his part of the bargain. It was time to leave, while there was still any light left. He shuddered, turned, and proceeded quickly after Shawn.

Silas was looking again at Adakhai. "I have need of your medicine, *Hatali*, and of your counsel."

The ancient one dipped his head. There would be none of the usual ceremony about this visit, Silas knew, just as he had the uncanny sensation that Adakhai had known all along what had been happening.

"You knew I was coming, *Hatali?*" he asked.

"For some weeks now, *Tsin-tzahn'jih Hatal'*, I have been waiting for you."

Adakhai's shrunken and withered frame was wrapped in a *yei*, a medicine man's blanket. His white hair hung over his shoulders, framing a countenance as wrinkled as a prune and quite as dark. His deep, very black eyes gazed at Pine.

"It was a bad dream, *Hatali*. It kept coming

272

to me again and again when I slept."

"You have need of *Nayenezg'ni,*" Adakhai intoned. "The Slayer of Enemies."

"I didn't then," Silas said. "I do now. Evil men have killed my only son."

"You did *then.*" Adakhai was emphatic. "The *tchindis,* the Dark-Walkers of the Night, cast their shadow upon you."

The ancient one picked up a stick at his side and stirred the hot coals in the fire. As he prodded them, flames danced back and forth among them, like sudden lightning. For a moment it seemed so real that it was as if a jagged ribbon of lightning was tearing across the sky itself, illumining a rider's contorted face as he opened up at those in front of him, sending off shots as fast as he could, their crackling echoes half lost in the sullen, droning boom of bright coals as they collapsed, rumbling deeply like thunder. *Silas heard it.* Right there, in the ancient shaman's hogan, in the dim light, he heard it. The sound of a painful grunt somewhere behind him. He wanted to turn but he couldn't take his eyes from the fire as there, where it glowed the brightest, he saw his son Noah rise up before him, slipping heavily from his saddle and pitching forward on his face.

"*Oh God . . . Noah!*" Pine gasped. "*Oh my God, not Noah!*"

Adakhai prodded the fire again and this time the flames leaped upward, shedding sparks and smoke. *It was the place of the trap.* There was the gorge, sculptured over eons, the black lava and the turrets of russet-colored sandstone, bizarre obsidian mosques tinted flaming crimson by the fire as if it were itself a dying sun. And the roar was in Silas's ears again. And it made the earth beneath him tremble. Before him now Pine could see the grand basaltic horseshoe with the driving water cascading over it as the fire leaped and quelled.

There were two boulders ahead, burning blue in the flames, and Pine was alone. He rolled forward onto his stomach, grasping at the hard earth of the hogan's floor with his fingers. He could see the man standing there on a narrow ledge deeply within the fire which now roared without restraint. The man's hands were raised and he lurched as he grabbed at an undergrowth of stubborn juniper. They were so close Pine could see the man's face, engulfed by the tempest of the fire. It was Massingale. Ben Massingale. And he was soaring out over the narrow defile. He became part of the cascading, roaring fire as he fell swiftly into oblivion.

The smoke began to cloud his vision. Pine realized that he was moaning aloud. He was terrified and he was trembling. The smoke swirled around him and began to rise toward the smoke hole at the top of the hogan. Silas fell silent. His eyes searched the gloom and finally came to rest on those deep, sunken sockets of Adakhai's and the shaman's eyes were so dark they seemed an empty, yawning vacuum.

"It *is* the place of the trap," Adakhai said then. "In fourteen suns, you shall be there, *Tsin-tzahn'jih Hatal'*, and *Nayenezga'ni* shall be there with you, and you will find the one who murdered your son. It is well. *Nayenezga'ni* has shown the way." He turned then toward the entrance to the hogan and in his ancient voice intoned *Has'tebaad* and his two granddaughters entered, drawing aside the hide covering which curtained the aperture, letting in a brief flash of dusky light.

"The sickness," Adakhai said now, "that we must cure, *Tsin-tzahn'jih Hatal'*, is not in your soul. But only in your body."

Chapter Twenty-Seven

The time it had taken Isom Rastrow to fetch a pillow from the small back bedroom and return with Reno Poteet and Black Ellis from their grisly job of placing Sarah Rogan's corpse on the bed proved sufficient for Lefty Price to lead his saddled horse from the barn and disappear around the far side from the house. By hitting leather in a southwesterly direction, he managed to keep the barn between his retreating figure and the Milton cabin until he was able to enter a clump of trees and vanish altogether from sight.

Now that a fire was going in the stove, Ellis, who acted as camp cook, proposed to begin the morning meal. Rastrow, joined by Poteet, was kneeling on the floor beside Massingale's unconscious form and, despite Kerry Lu's plea to leave her father alone, they were trying to revive the man. Poteet rose to get the water bucket which stood on the sink board while Rastrow chafed Massingale's hands.

Ellis said he would have to go out to the barn to get some of the supplies packed in the wagon. Neither Poteet nor Rastrow commented on his remark, so intent were they on reviving Massingale. However, it was as a consequence of Black Ellis's trip to the barn that Lefty Price's disappearance was discovered as soon as it was.

This latest reversal seemed to snap Isom Rastrow's nerve. It was not something obvious at once to either Poteet or Ellis, despite the years they had ridden with the man. But it was there, nonetheless, a rippling nervous tension far behind his eyes and his movements quickened. Leaving Kerry Lu beside her father, Rastrow signed for Poteet to join him and Ellis as he led the way back to the barn. A hurried search of the interior confirmed that, indeed, Black was right. Price had taken his horse and ridden out.

This move precipitated a change in plans, one which Rastrow outlined to the other two men as they stood, huddled, in the drafty barn. After breakfast and Kerry Lu had quieted down, she was to be seized and tied up, then taken out to the barn where she was to be kept while Rastrow with Massingale tied to a spare horse would head out toward Twin Falls. Poteet and Ellis could pleasure themselves with the girl, if they were so inclined, but she was not to be killed. Instead, once they had finished with her, she was to be tied up again and left in the barn alive.

Sarah Rogan's body was to be placed in the old rocking chair that stood in one corner of the main room of the cabin and she was to be set out on the porch as if resting and enjoying the scenery. Ellis was to work his way up the rock outcropping behind the cabin so he could keep an eye on the road leading into the ranch yard. Poteet was to station himself in a small grove of alder trees beside the road just before it turned into the ranch yard and wait for Rogan's arrival. That's where he was to be relieved of the ransom money. If anybody was with him, Ellis was to shoot them from his vantage point high up on the rock outcropping. If Rogan was alone, both men were to be on their way before he arrived at the cabin porch and discovered that his wife was dead.

Rastrow would take with him, split in packs on his horse and the one to which Massingale was to be tied, enough provisions to see him through for two weeks or more. Ellis and Poteet were each to ride out in separate directions and were to do their best to obscure their trails in case there was any pursuit from town. Each was to take provisions sufficient to see them through that week and another when they would all meet up at Twin Falls. By that time Massingale would either be dead and his body disposed of, or he would have been forced by Rastrow to tell where he had buried the bank loot. By then enough time would have passed that they could come back together to locate the loot and finally be shut of the district for good.

It was a good plan. They all agreed. Rastrow and Ellis would have to trust Poteet not to run out with the ransom money, but he knew, as well as they did, the consequences of such a play. What strength they had would be preserved only by sticking together.

The only hitch they encountered was Kerry Lu's resistance when, following the meal, Poteet slipped up behind her and dallied a rope over her shoulders. She fought and screamed and clawed at him until Rastrow had to pacify her with a fist to the jaw which knocked her out briefly. By the time she regained consciousness, she was bound and gagged and lying in a mound of hay in the barn.

Massingale's breathing was shallow. Rastrow was doubtful that the man would make it through alive, but he salved his conscience with the thought that at least his plan would spare Kerry Lu's life. Her terror, her grief, and the hatred mingled with horror at the brutality to which she had been exposed, continued to trouble Rastrow long after he was on the trail toward Twin Falls, leading behind him Massingale's horse snubbed by means of a lariat to the pummel of his saddle. Most of all he wanted to be far away from Jake Milton's cabin and barn. If anything more was to go wrong, it would happen to those he had left behind. The money Rogan was supposed to bring would be enough to keep them there. If they didn't make it, Isom Rastrow would still have his freedom.

By the white man's standards, Gage Cameron was a wealthy man. His discovery of a cache of gold had allowed him to alter the life of poverty and frustration which long had been the Cameron lot. His father, Mungo Cameron, a Scottish immigrant who had wallowed in years of sustained drunkenness following the death of his Navajo wife, had given up drink. Able to afford to stock his sheep ranch, he had transformed his life into building a substantial legacy for his children. Gage's younger brother, Ran, had stayed on and was now foreman over a half dozen herders. Amber, Gage's younger sister, who had kept house for the family in former days, had decided to attend a finishing school in the East now that the family could afford it, but her letters home seemed to indicate second thoughts, homesickness, and frustration over not being accepted by the other girls because she was a half-breed.

The only way Gage could solve the dilemma of his own life had been to make a final choice between the two worlds into which he had been born. He had decided to leave most of the money behind with his father who was a white man and who knew how to prosper on the white man's road. Marrying a former slave and a black woman only increased the prejudice which Gage had always felt among white men so he and Opal, married in a Navajo ceremony, had found their share of happiness living at Adakhai's Navajo encampment.

Gage and Opal had tried to have a child, but it had not happened. When Opal returned from Grafton with Baby Hope, Gage at once took the small child to his heart. For him, as for Opal, it made their world complete.

Hearing the commotion outside Adakhai's hogan, Gage had left Opal with Baby Hope and gone to investigate. He recognized Shawn Massingale as she and Lefty Price stepped outside the hogan and into the fading twilight.

Nor were they the only visitors that late afternoon to the camp. Santiago Cruz and his wife Mariana, one of the *Dineh,* had also ridden in from the direction of Grafton. Mariana had heavy, stolid features, and was dressed in traditional Navajo garb accentuated by a brightly colored Mexican serape. Two of her sisters lived here and there was a reunion in progress. Santiago must have seen Shawn Massingale emerge from Adakhai's hogan at the same time Gage Cameron did, approaching from the opposite direction. They converged on the distraught woman as Lefty Price drew back from them.

Gage Cameron was not blessed with the appealing features of his younger brother and sister who had more of the beauty of their mother. His face was craggy like his father's, even ugly by some standards, but his smile was winning. Shawn embraced him and then embraced Santiago. She began almost at once to tell both of them what she had learned from Price as to the whereabouts of Ben and Kerry Lu. It was then that she became aware of the distance between where she was and Price who had made it over to where he had tied his horse.

"The joodge has made me a deeputy, Señora," Cruz said. "I am to search for where thees hombres have taken Ben and Kerry Lu. I brought Mariana here for a visit and was to continue searching the Neversummers."

"Are ye gone gyte?" Shawn snapped at Lefty Price, fixing her glance on him in the shadows near his horse. The other two followed with their eyes the direction in which she was looking.

"That was the deal, ma'am," Price said,

now nervously holding onto the reins of his gray. "You and old Mr. Pine said I could pull out once I got you all here."

Price had been peering at Shawn through the dim light and so did not see Cruz draw his six-gun.

"Thees is wun of thees men I am look for," the Mexican said. "Hee ees part of Rastrow's gang."

"Na any more," Shawn said, reaching out and resting her right hand on Santiago's gun arm. "Without him, we couldn't have made it here, nor would I know where to find Ben and Kerry Lu."

"If they're still there, Shawn," Gage Cameron said soberly. He looked over toward Lefty Price. "What do you think the gang will do once they discover you've pulled out?" he asked.

"Cain't rightly say," Price answered. The truth was he hadn't given that question any thought since he had made certain that he wasn't being pursued.

"Please, Santiago, put it away," Shawn said. "We gave this man our sworn troth."

Amid the smoke blowing from the cook fires and from the smoke-holes of the hogans of the camp and the gloom, Price couldn't be certain, but he recognized the silhouette somehow. Opal Cameron had silently approached the group assembled outside Adakhai's hogan and, as she came closer, Price's doubt increased to a certainty. It was the fierce black Navajo who had nearly killed him back there at the Crowley shack.

"I gotta go," Price said. His voice had a slightly hysterical overtone and he bunched the reins in his hands as he raised his foot to the stirrup.

"What's he doing here?" Opal asked suddenly, causing everyone to swing around in her direction.

Cruz shook off Shawn's restraining hand and aimed his six-gun at Price.

"Don' do it, *Señor*. Even in thees light, I can eshoot you before you are in thee saddle."

Price was confused by what to do and his gelding was beginning to stamp, jittery perhaps by the unfamiliar surroundings and the enclave of strangers, to say nothing of Price's own nervousness.

Shawn dashed forward and turned her back to Price, facing the others.

"We swore a troth to this man," she said sharply. "He has the right to leave unharmed and who's to bear the wyte of it, if our troth is broken?"

"You know where you're going?" Gage Cameron asked, putting his arm around Opal and looking straight at Price. "It's almost

284

dark. Do you know your way about in the Neversummers."

"Enough to get a sight clear outa here," Price said.

Shawn now had turned toward Lefty.

"Ye are safe, Mister Price. These people are my friends. They sha'n't harm ye."

"Mebbe," said Price, still tugging at his gelding, trying to quiet it. "But I had a run-in with that black Injun once afore, and once was enough."

Opal laughed and Gage was grinning. Cruz still held his six-gun on the man. It was then, from within Adakhai's hogan, that they all heard the unmistakable voice of Silas Pine, moaning. The terror in it gripped them all.

"Who is in there with *el viejo, Señora?*" Santiago asked in a hushed voice.

A brisk wind had come up, biting cold, as Horace Rogan had held the reins of the smart pair of matched blacks as his buggy had pulled out of Grafton and the town receded behind him. He almost had to smile to himself when he thought of the failure of the pursuing posse to get farther than a mile out of town two nights before — and with no particular hindrance from him. The wet snow falling, the muddiness of the road, the disorganization of the posse, and the fear the horses had for the

285

lighted torches had all conspired to have everything called off and the posse had returned to town grumbling and in a dour mood.

Rogan knew that Judge Tabor had sworn in Santiago Cruz as a deputy marshal and that he and his wife Mariana had headed out to the Navajo village. Cruz intended to use Adakhai's camp as his headquarters while he searched the Neversummers in an effort to locate where Rastrow and his men might have holed up. His chances of finding them would have been a lot better if he had headed north toward the Milton place. As it was, having headed south, they would be far away before long.

All in all, the despair and nausea which had overcome him in the dark stable when Isom Rastrow had told him the truth of what had happened to Obadiah had passed as he had time to think it over and arrived at the decision that by paying Rastrow this $10,000 his hands were finally clean. True, Obbie had betrayed him; but in a very real way he had no less betrayed his son. He did not know if Sarah would ever be able to forgive him if she were to learn the truth, but he was definitely not going to be the one to tell her and it was unlikely that Rastrow or his men would let anything slip. What inner torment could not be assuaged by paying off Rastrow would come, he sincerely hoped, by the renewed attention and devotion he would henceforth shower on Sarah.

His obsession with the bank and with accumulating wealth had distracted him too often and too much from his duties as a husband and, possibly, as a father. Nothing could be done to bring Obbie back. If he had gone bad as a result of his father's neglect, both had paid a dear price for it. Horace must now make it up to Sarah. What remained to them of their lives could be made more into what it should have been from the beginning. Having so long cuddled Baby Hope, he was surprised at himself. The baby's color had not bothered him in the least. He knew he had felt Baby Hope's father was inferior by virtue of race and background. His principal motive in lending him money had been his expectation of being able to foreclose eventually. But Baby Hope, so full of life, of innocence, so in need of care and nurture, had stolen into his heart in a way that had not even happened when his own son had been born more than twenty years ago.

"Hold it right there, Rogan."

The peremptory voice broke into the banker's placid daydreaming. He tugged on the reins and pulled up the team. The sun was creeping behind the tallest of the Neversummers and the light in the valley where Jake Milton had had his ranch had begun to fade. The speaker sounded like Reno Poteet and that is who it proved to be as the mounted man eased his horse out of an alder grove and rode slowly toward Rogan's buggy. Up ahead, in the dimming light, he could make out the barn and Milton's cabin. There seemed to be someone sitting on a rocking chair on the front porch. At this distance in this light, and with his failing vision for distant objects, however, he could not be sure who the person might be.

"Where's Rastrow?" Rogan demanded as Poteet reined in alongside the buggy.

"Gone. Don't ask me where."

"No, of course, I understand. And Massingale?"

"Went with Isom. Thet's your wife waitin' fer yuh up on the porch. She's been tol' not to move. Black's up there in the rocks behind the cabin with a rifle. She knows better than try and leave the porch."

"But it's so chilly," Rogan protested.

"Cain't yuh see she's got her coat on?" Poteet said reassuringly, and then added: "See yuh came by yourself as you were told. Got the money?"

"Right here in this satchel," Rogan said, indicating the black bag near his left foot on the floorboard of the buggy.

"Hand it out then, Horace," Reno said. "Remember, Black's got his sights trained on yuh."

Poteet leaned over and took the proffered satchel from the banker's hand. Rogan's other, his left, still held the reins.

"It's all there, as agreed," Rogan assured the man.

"Figgered it would be," Poteet said, looping the satchel onto the saddlehorn of his Texas rig.

"Kerry Lu?" Rogan asked.

"You'll find her in the barn, all ready and waitin' fer yuh."

Reno smiled, but in the half light it was more of a leer. Without saying another word, he turned his horse away and disappeared again into the alder grove. Horace Rogan snapped the reins smartly and the team proceeded quickly up the winding road leading to the ranch compound and the porch on which his wife was sitting.

It was pre-arranged between Poteet and Ellis that they would meet briefly after the money was taken from Rogan. As Poteet vanished from sight in the alder grove, he headed northeast and then north, circling around the Milton place so as to approach Black Ellis from where he was concealed at the top of the rock outcropping.

Reno had tied his horse to a deadfall near where Ellis had sequestered his horse and was mounting the rock outcropping from the rear to reach the niche where Ellis was stationed when he heard it. The sound was a retort, but not from a rifle or even a large caliber six-gun. Just a short, sharp little pop, and then silence.

Ellis squirmed around and watched Poteet crawl carefully from the narrow defile to where he was perched. There was a grin on his face.

"Was that a shot I heard?" Poteet asked, as he slipped down beside Ellis who was kneeling on one knee and holding his rifle in his right hand.

"Yeah, it was a shot." Ellis looked at the black satchel Poteet was carrying. "Did you count it?"

"Not yet. I thought we could do it together up here and then head back about a quarter of a mile to camp. We can split up in the morning. But mebbe not. Who was doin' the shootin'."

"Rogan," Ellis answered. "You should have seen him. He leaps out of that buggy of his and runs almost up the steps of the porch, before he stops cold. Even at this distance I could tell he saw somethin' wasn't right. Then he goes over to the body and collapses on his knees. It looked to me like he must have been cryin'. I thought he was just gonna stay that way till the sun set, but no. After a few minutes, wiping his eyes with a handkerchief, he stumbles down off the porch and goes over to the barn. He eases himself in careful like and was in there a couple of minutes before he comes sidlin' out again. His arms were saggin' at his sides and he looked all tuckered. He goes up to the porch steps, sets down, and pulls out what must have been one of those little Derringers tinhorns like. I saw the sun glint on it as he put it to his forehead."

"Rogan shot himself?" Poteet asked in astonishment.

"Naw, no such luck. He must of lost the stomach for it at the last minute because the shot went wild and he flung the little gun into the road in front of him. Now he's back with the old lady, settin' himself in the rockin' chair and cuddlin' her body."

Poteet opened the clasp and showed the satchel's contents to Ellis.

"Want to count it here, or wait until we make camp."

"After we make camp suits me," Ellis said, coming slowly to his feet. "Sittin' here and thinkin' about that gutless Rogan makes me sick."

The two began edging their way up the narrow defile and then down to where their horses were tethered.

Lefty Price never really knew exactly how it had happened. For a while back there, it had looked as if he wouldn't get out of that Injun camp without shooting someone and likely get shot himself. But it hadn't happened that way. Shawn had won Opal over to her side about Price and then the two women had proposed they all hold a pow-wow in the Cameron hogan. What had broken the spell, Price opined, had been Silas Pine's moaning inside the old Injun medicine man's hogan.

Price had heard about such things in his youth, about how religious men sometimes cast devils out of a person. It must be something like that happening to old Pine in there with that old medicine man. It had been eerie and repulsive at the same time and he was glad just to get away from there. That Opal was an outstanding cook, black Injun or not, Price had to admit. Santiago had finally sheathed his gun and he and Gage Cameron had been full of questions about the Milton layout and the best way to approach it. Even at that, he would be heading south instead of north had it not been for Shawn Massingale. She had been so determined to get her man and her daughter back that there was no way she was going to be left behind at the Navajo camp.

Under those circumstances, and because of the way he felt about everything else that had happened, Lefty had volunteered to lead Shawn, Santiago, and Gage to the Milton place. Santiago had been there once before. Shawn had been there twice. Gage had never been there. But none of the three of them knew Rastrow and the others the way he did. Assuming the three men were still there, it would have been suicidal to ride in on them. And there was no telling what might happen to Kerry Lu and Massingale if it came to a pitched battle. It had been Lefty's suggestion, therefore, that they should slip around to the north and approach the place from the rear.

Gage had provided fresh mounts for Price, Shawn, and Santiago from his own string. Mariana, Santiago's squaw, had been summoned to old Adakhai's hogan. She had something of a reputation for her healing abilities. Price had seen her and Shawn engaged in a short but passionate conversation just before they pulled out.

The journey had been a long one and the group had moved with deliberation in order to spare the horses. Gage knew the way down from the Neversummers even better than Santiago did. Shawn rode beside the Mexican. Lefty took the lead after they hit the flat ground of the valley and were heading in the direction of the Milton ranch.

They circled around at least a mile north of the place before they turned the horses and slowly proceeded toward the distant rock outcropping which stood slightly to the side and behind the cabin and barn. It was early dawn and they could see the terrain in front of them well enough to be able to spot the dry camp of Black Ellis and Reno Poteet.

Price couldn't be certain it was they, nor did he know what they could possibly be doing camped out like that, but he did recognize their horses. Gage, Santiago, and Price all dismounted, leaving Shawn behind to watch their mounts.

Gage disappeared into the underbrush. It was his intention to creep up on the other side of the camp. Lefty and Santiago split up and came in, each at an angle. When Price had drawn near enough to distinguish who was in the camp, Reno Poteet had already risen and was adding wood to the little fire. Lefty had drawn his six-gun and he drew a bead on Poteet.

"Ees far enough, *Señores*," Santiago Cruz's voice cracked sharply in the early dawn cold. "Don' mak' any fonny moves."

"It's that goddamned greaser!" Black Ellis roared and bounded from his covers, his six-gun drawn.

Cruz's bullet hit him square in the middle and he was driven backward, falling in a heap on the very blankets from which he had just risen so abruptly. Poteet had his gun out by this time.

"Don't try it," Lefty called, and moved slightly into view so Reno would see that he was covered.

Poteet's expression was not so much shock at seeing Price as it was instant rage. His gun spewed flame and smoke three times in Price's direction before two bullets, one from Cruz's six-gun and one from Gage's Winchester, cut him down where he stood.

Chapter Twenty-Eight

Mariana Cruz was staying with her sister Estsan' Ad'le-hi. They were of the *Hahl tsói* clan. This name had been corrupted by the white man's influence so that it was now known among the whites as Hosteen, the Navajo word for head of the family and not for meadow — after which this clan had once been named in the dim past. Mariana's and Estsan' Ad'le-hi's three brothers worked for Gage Cameron's father on his sheep ranch as herders while their wives in the village owned their own herds of sheep. Mariana's name was of Spanish origin.

Silas Pine remembered her vaguely from the time when he had lived briefly with the Navajos, but they had come to be close friends over the past few days while Mariana had ministered to his wounds. Pine was now able to walk, to sit, and he had even ridden a horse around the village this morning. It had been exhausting, but he had done it.

When Santiago Cruz and Gage Cameron rode in, they went at once to Estsan' Ad'le-hi's hogan after learning that this was where Pine was recovering. They joined Pine, sitting solemnly around the fire, their legs crossed. He was anxious to hear what happened but he made no effort to hurry either man.

"Good and bad, *amigo*," Cruz said at last. "Kerry Lu, she ees alive, but she was badly treated by those *hombres*."

"Raped?" Pine asked.

"*Si*. Many times I have the fear, *amigo*."

"And the gang?"

"The *hombres* calling themselves Reno and Black are keeled, *muerte*, *amigo*. I eshoot one, Gage and I thee other."

"Rastrow?"

"He wasn't there," Gage Cameron said, speaking for the first time. "He had apparently left the previous day and he took Ben Massingale with him. That much we could determine from the tracks. I tried to follow them but lost them on rocky ground. I may be half Navajo, Silas, but I can read better English than I can follow sign. I'm sorry."

"I have a good idea where they are," Silas said, and was then silent.

"Shawn," said Cruz, "she esay to me that she does not want anyone to follow after them. Ben may wee'll escape on his own. She wants for you to com' an' estay with her an' Kerry Lu when you have your health."

"She told Mariana the same thing before

she left," Pine said. "Not about following Rastrow and Massingale, but about how I should come to their place."

"It will be all right, Silas," Gage Cameron said. "It's hers now, free and clear."

"How'd that happen?" Pine asked.

"*Señor* Rogan, *amigo,* hee gave it bac' to her," Cruz said. "As a reeward, because the ransohm mahney he brought was return' to heem. The two who were keeled had it at their camp. Hees wife, the *Señora* Rogan, she ees *muerte.*"

"That's what Lefty Price said," Pine recalled.

"*Si,* an' now so ees Lefty . . . almost."

"Almost?" Pine asked.

"Like you, Silas," Cruz said. "He should be dead. He has three bullets in him, but yet he lives. For how long, there no ees telling. But I went to Grafton and brought Doc Whitelaws back with me and the doc, he says *Señor* Price have thee chance, even if only a very, very sleem one."

"I hope he makes it," said Pine. "In his way, he is a good man. And Rogan?"

"Hees heart, she ees brok'," said Cruz. "I 'ave neever seen sooch a sad man beefore. He gave bac' *Señora* Shawn her place and thee place of *Señor* Milton and he offered Gage thee Crowley place an' that of *Señor*

Blayde for what they do for Baby Hope."

Pine said nothing but the expression on his face was skeptical.

"I know how you feel, Silas," Gage said. "But the offer was honest enough. He only asks that we let him visit Baby Hope once in a while to see how she is doing."

"Where is Shawn Massingale now?" Pine asked.

"At her place," Gage said. "We took her and Kerry Lu there after I came back with the doc."

"The estages, they rohn smoothly once more," Cruz said, and smiled grimly.

"You think you really know where Rastrow and Massingale have gone?" Gage asked.

"Yes," Pine said. "I'm pretty sure. I rode a little today. I'll ride more tomorrow. Then I will go after them."

"Alone?" Gage asked hesitantly.

"Reckon."

"Ohh, no, *amigo*. You canno' go without your frien' Santiago."

"Nor without me," Gage said.

Pine sat quietly for several moments, pondering. His face was gaunted. The whiskers, unshaven for days, were wiry and patched with white. Then he looked from one to the other.

"This is the way it must be," he said slowly.

"I ride point. Santiago, you can follow me, but only at a distance. Gage, you follow Santiago, but again at a distance, and you bring the pack horse with our supplies. If I am downed. . . ." He paused to tap his chest above his heart softly with a clenched fist. "I will know that you two will do your best to finish it."

"You mean," said Cruz, "feenish heem . . . Rastrow?"

Pine nodded.

The wind was blowing, harsh and cold, upon Silas Pine's back. The pain had become a dull throb and his flannel shirt adhered to him as if glued there by blood or sweat, maybe both. It had been insane to try it, but Pine only gritted his teeth and pressed on.

The trail turned and twisted between the volcanic upthrusts and monoliths of black lava. The roar of the falls had been increasing for some miles now although he still couldn't see the crashing, churning water. Turrets of sandstone russet in color, bizarre obsidian mosques, tinted flaming crimson in the dying sun, were all just as he had seen them so many times in his dream.

Coming around a lava outcropping, withered by eons of erosion, Pine suddenly beheld the gorge beneath Twin Falls off to his left,

300

and precipitously down. The earth was trembling and his horse, a sure-footed Navajo gelding from Adakhai's string, was becoming increasingly uneasy. A heavy mist obscured the river below with thick clouds of vapor. Ahead in the distance, the water turned into crimson flames by the declining sun, tons and tons of water plunging downward from the basaltic horseshoe that was Twin Falls into the engulfing spray.

The roar of the water was so great that Pine never heard the rifle shot. He felt something tug at his buckskin jacket and knew the lead had missed him. Reining his horse swiftly back, he retreated quickly behind the black lava outcropping he had just rounded. Slowly, somewhat painfully, he dismounted and tied the gelding to the limb of a juniper. Taking his rifle from the scabbard, he plunged into the narrow rock defile that seemed to parallel the trail along the rim. He would have to move quickly. The light would soon be gone.

The trembling of the earth increased as Pine worked his way closer to the falls. The defile had led out onto the rim. There was a rock outcropping and a ledge slightly back and above the falls. That was probably the place from which the shot had come. By edging upward along a narrow slot, Pine hoped he could come out from behind the rocks overlooking the outcropping and the ledge.

Once he slipped badly and his rifle went clattering down the notch. Pine did not stop to retrieve it. He still had the Colt in his holster. It was just as well anyway since he now had to use both his hands to prevent him from slipping off the smooth, round surfaces of the rocks. The whole area was slick from spray and mist emanating from the torrential pounding of the falls.

He came out just above the outcropping, slipping and sliding up a fissure in the lava, his hulking form flitting like a shadow from rock to rock, cleft to cleft. The rocks had torn his coat nearly to ribbons and had ripped chunks from his flesh. His body trembled as much as did the earth, from the strain of it.

There were two boulders ahead and Pine crawled between them, one jutting out above, one below. He slid out from behind the top one, his boots slipping and sliding on the polished, wet shale beneath his feet. He paused because he could see a figure standing there on a narrow ledge beneath him that jutted outward about six feet from the canyon wall. The surface of the black lava was shiny and glistened darkly in the vanishing light.

Pine reached back and drew out his Colt. In his dream he had never seen the face of this man. In the fire inside Adakhai's hogan the face had been that of Ben Massingale.

Bracing his back, shot through now with tremors of agony, the ground trembling underfoot until it seemed actually to shudder uncontrollably, the roar of the falls enveloping all other sound, Pine peered into the dim gloom to make out the man's face. The sweat and blood were running down his back now and sweat even oozed through the blood which had caked on his right hand, holding the Colt.

The man was swaying on that narrow ledge. He had a rifle in one hand and a six-gun in the other, pointed downward. As Pine watched, the sweat and mist now threatening to blur his vision, the rifle slid from pale fingers, then the six-gun, hitting against the steep side of the canyon without a sound, and bouncing downward into oblivion. The man raised his bare head and Pine saw his face at last, just as he collapsed suddenly and went off the ledge into space.

For almost a week now, Ben Massingale had spent most of his time, awake or asleep, tied hand and foot. Rastrow said little to him after that first day's torture. He had evidently convinced the outlaw that there never had been any money taken from the bank. The torture had stopped as had the talk. They then had traveled nearly two hundred miles overland

and had been camped here six days.

Twice a day, Rastrow untied him long enough to relieve himself and to get around the meager grub shoved before him in a tin plate. The rest of the time he was left mostly to himself while Rastrow took up his perch outside the lava fold in which he had set up camp, waiting, watching the trail. Massingale knew only that Reno Poteet and Black Ellis were expected. He had no clue as to what had delayed them. He could see Rastrow's increasing irritation. He also knew that as soon as the others did come his time was over.

Ben thought of Shawn in those many long hours. He thought of very little else but Shawn, and Kerry Lu, and the life that might have been theirs, but for his foolishness. He should never have listened to Obbie Rogan's scheme. It was fated to fail, as everything Obbie Rogan had ever done had failed.

With Kerry Lu sleeping in the same room, he and Shawn had been able to make love very little. But that didn't mean Ben couldn't remember what it had once been like and be happy that they had done it so many times when they'd had the chance.

Ben's soul was dark when he thought of Kerry Lu left alone at the Milton ranch with those two vermin. He feared what was likely to have happened and it had made him battle the ropes which encased him. The problem was that he had been growing weaker by the day. Once he might have been able to break those bonds. Now just rubbing them against a sharp edge of lava wall exhausted him after only a few moments.

He would have to do it soon, or forever abandon hope. Rastrow had packed up much of the camp today. It was obviously the last day he was going to remain here waiting. With a shuddering breath, Ben had worked the wrist rope against the razor-like lava.

He was too dazed at first to realize that his hands were free. Then, with clumsy fingers, he attacked the ropes around his ankles. His wrists and hands were bleeding and his fingers could barely function when, with an explosion of despairing strength, knowing it was his last bid, he undid the last knot and could pull the hempen cord away.

Ben found his own six-gun in the saddlebag where he knew Rastrow kept it. Pain by now was roaring through his head, but a greater roaring filled his consciousness. He felt the dampness of the eternal spray as he crept out from the outcropping.

The greenish haze of foam hung above the red rocks like a thick fog and the roaring waters seemed as much inside Ben's head as outside of it. He could make out the figure of

Rastrow standing in front of him, his eyes carefully scanning the trail below and the rocks of the canyon wall, his rifle poised in his hands, ready to fire the instant he saw his prey. Clutching his own six-gun in his hand, Massingale fired point blank, right straight into Rastrow's back.

The man crumpled before him. Ben edged forward and bent over to pick up the rifle where Rastrow had dropped it when he fell. He had moved forward, unable to hear his own footsteps, holding his six-gun tightly. He had changed hands with the six-gun when he had picked up the rifle. Suddenly, he could not be sure from where, a big, top-heavy figure loomed up in front of him and a gun flamed right in his eyes. Ben felt the stunning pain of lead rocking into him. He staggered backwards, turning, trying not to lose his footing, stumbling to the edge of the ridge over the gorge. He could feel the life draining out of him as he pivoted slowly, his back to the roaring falls. The rifle slid from his right hand and then the revolver fell from his left hand. Swaying backward on uncertain legs he turned his face up toward the sky. There, just above him, hunched over in a declivity, was the battered, anguished face of Silas Pine.

As Ben Massingale slid over the slick edge

of the precipice, Pine was stunned to see on his face what was unmistakably a smile. Baffled for a moment, Pine squeezed his eyelids shut, to force out the sweat and spray. He rubbed his left sleeve, what was left of it, across his eyes, and opened them again. Staggering now into view, hobbling, holding a hand far around against one side, was Isom Rastrow. His eyes moved from the edge of the gorge upward in Pine's direction.

Rastrow may have screamed. Pine knew for a fact that he did, although he could not hear his own voice as he did it. The spray beating on his face as the rain had that night when Noah had been shot down, Pine screamed and fired at the same time. Rastrow's body tilted for an instant, caught as if in suspension, and then slipped over backwards into the greenish hell of the gorge. Pine stood transfixed as Rastrow, rather than hurtling swiftly out of sight as Massingale had, seemed to arc out over the narrow defile. His body came very close to the farther south wall as it careened, then the green arteries of churning water suddenly engulfed him.

Pine didn't want to look down, but he couldn't help himself. His vision was clouded by the mist. He was screaming again, but the sound was lost in the primeval crashing thunder of the falls. Then, the enveloping roar of the falls all he could hear, Pine himself sagged down on the lava ridge, head thrust forward, his body spent.

It had been Santiago Cruz who had found him. Pine's body, slick with blood and water, had been gradually sliding down the loose shale from the crevice where he had first fallen and he was very near to the lip before Cruz was able to pull him back. The twilight had turned to grayish blue and nightfall was near.

Pine's two companions then had located Rastrow's and Massingale's horses and had loaded up what was left of the camp gear and supplies. Gage Cameron set out the next morning alone. Two days and two nights Santiago Cruz stayed with Pine at a camp they made a few miles from the falls, where the roar was only heard dimly. For a man who had been so near death so many times, Pine's overall physical condition, notwithstanding what he told the Mexican about his fatal heart condition, must have been truly extraordinary that he was thus able, once again, to restore himself.

They took their time on the ride back to Grafton in Wyoming which is where Silas Pine now wanted to go. Under ordinary conditions, the ride might have required five days.

They made it on the seventh day after they had set out.

It was near dusk as Pine led his horse the short distance outside of town to the Grafton cemetery. Dismounting, the light bathing him and the ground in red flames, Pine limped slowly among the graves. He had left Santiago at the livery stable. He had wanted to be alone.

Pine could not help thinking about all the recent graves that had been dug here. Noah had not been the first casualty. There had been two of the ranchers who had tried to rob the bank, and Obbie Rogan. Then Noah, and Sam Crowley. Then Aurelia Crowley. Finally, Sarah Rogan.

The bile tasted bitter in his mouth as Silas paused before Noah's grave. It would have been impossible to have found Ben Massingale's body even if he and Cruz had searched for it. Ben would not be buried here, but Silas would see to it that there was a monument for him.

His head bowed, his hat in his hand, Pine had been standing there silently at Noah's grave for some time when he heard the sound of a step on the crushed stones behind him. He looked up slowly and in the gloom recognized the craggy, withered, lined face of Rawina. He was about to say something about leaving him undisturbed in his mourning when she spoke.

"Silas?"

"Yes."

"Noah came to me that night before you set out after Ben Massingale and Sam Crowley. He told me about having dinner with you and how you two had talked."

Pine stood silently, his body rigid.

"He . . . ," her voice cracked, but she went on, "he told me that it somehow seemed all right to him. At last. He said he didn't hate you any more. For all the nights that he had wept and couldn't sleep. All the nights he had ached wanting you to come back and be with him. He . . . he said that for the first time since you had left home he felt . . . he *knew* that he loved you, that he had always loved you, that . . . maybe now . . . you could be family again."

Rawina's eyes faced Pine, the deeply slanting sun reflected in them. Perhaps for that reason her eyes fluttered as she finished speaking. Surely for that reason she could no longer see his face clearly, nor the large tears which rolled down his cheeks, nor the anguished sorrow that was so great he had been struck dumb by it.

She turned and retreated back toward town. Silas stared after her for several long moments.

The tears were still streaking his face as he limped over to the gelding and slowly mounted, holding the left stirrup so he could awkwardly get his foot into it.

Mostly she had been silent since their return. Sometimes Kerry Lu had cried and then Shawn had been there to hold her. Even when she sobbed, she did not speak. Shawn feared that Kerry Lu might never speak again. Gage Cameron had come by and told them both that Ben was dead. It made the silence between them even more agonizing.

It surprised her, therefore, all the more when, while preparing supper, she heard Kerry Lu speak to her from the front porch where she had been sitting most of the afternoon.

"Ma, someone's coming," her voice called into the house.

Shawn rushed from the stove to the doorway. Her heart was in her throat.

"It's Silas Pine, Ma. I can see him clearly from here."

Shawn had no idea what possessed her daughter. One listless moment after another, with nary more than a sigh or a sob to mark the passing days, and now there she was bounding out into the lingering twilight, running to greet Silas Pine.

There were tears in Shawn's eyes. Words she had spoken over and over to Kerry Lu since their return came back to her. "You and I have to go on from here, Kerry Lu. People are made that way. They have to go on living."

Then, with a toss of her head, she followed Kerry Lu out into the lengthening shadows darkening the compound.

T.V. Olsen was born in Rhinelander, Wisconsin, where he continued to live all his life. "My childhood was unremarkable except for an inordinate preoccupation with Zane Grey and Edgar Rice Burroughs." He had originally planned to be a comic strip artist but the stories he came up with proved far more interesting to him, and compelling, than any desire to illustrate them. Having read such accomplished Western authors as Les Savage, Jr., Luke Short, and Elmore Leonard, he began writing his first Western novel while a junior in high school. He couldn't find a publisher for it until he rewrote it after graduating from college with a Bachelor's degree from the University of Wisconsin at Stevens Point in 1955 and sent it to an agent. It was accepted by Ace Books and was published in 1956 as HAVEN OF THE HUNTED.

Olsen went on to become one of the most widely respected and widely read authors of Western fiction in the second half of the 20th Century. Even early works such as HIGH LAWLESS and GUNSWIFT are brilliantly plotted with involving characters and situations and a simple, powerfully evocative style. Olsen went on to write such important Western novels as THE STALKING MOON and ARROW IN THE SUN which were made into classic Western films as well, the former starring Gregory Peck and the latter under the title SOLDIER BLUE starring Candice Bergen. His novels have been translated into numerous European languages, including French, Spanish, Italian, Swedish, Serbo-Croatian, and Czech.

The second edition of TWENTIETH CENTURY WESTERN WRITERS concluded that "with the right press Olsen could command the position currently enjoyed by the late Louis L'Amour as America's most popular and foremost author of traditional Western novels." His novel THE GOLDEN CHANCE (Gold Medal, 1992) won the Golden Spur Award from the Western Writers of America in 1993.

Suddenly and unexpectedly, death claimed him in his sleep on the afternoon of July 13, 1993. His work, however, will surely abide. Any Olsen novel is guaranteed to combine drama and memorable characters with an au-
hentic background of historical fact and an
urate portrayal of Western terrain.

We hope you have enjoyed this Large Print book. Other Thorndike Press or Chivers Press Large Print books are available at your library or directly from the publishers. For more information about current and upcoming titles, please call or write, without obligation, to:

Thorndike Press
P.O. Box 159
Thorndike, Maine 04986
USA
Tel. (800) 223-6121 (U.S. & Canada)
In Maine call collect: (207) 948-2962

OR

Chivers Press Limited
Windsor Bridge Road
Bath BA2 3AX
England
Tel. (0225) 335336

All our Large Print titles are designed for easy reading, and all our books are made to last.